The buzz about *The Social Hour*?

"*Wood's books are always good, but her new Decklin Kilgarry series exceeds expectation. The Social Hour is great!*"

—Karen Campbell

"*As with all of Wood's mystery books, there's always a twist or two, and I never see them coming! The mark of an excellent book, I think!*"

—Randall Carpenter

"*Once again, Faith Wood delivers! On par with her other award-winning books, The Social Hour transports mystery readers into intrigue like no other!*"

—M. Oswald

"*I've read all of Wood's books, and I thoroughly enjoyed them—The Social Hour is no exception!*"

—Chris C.

"*I wasn't big on reading until I read Faith Wood's first mystery book—now, I'm completely hooked, and I can never wait for the next one. Loved The Social Hour!*"

—M. W. McCall

"*If I were stuck on an island, I'd want a Faith Wood mystery— and my glasses! The Social Hour in particular . . .*"

—Dalton Hemmings

"*The Social Hour is such a great book—and, like all of Wood's books, I couldn't put it down!*"

—Mikala G.

THE SOCIAL HOUR

A DECKLIN KILGARRY SUSPENSE MYSTERY—BOOK 4

The Social Hour

A Decklin Kilgarry Suspense Mystery—Book 4

FAITH WOOD

Wood Media
British Columbia, Canada

ISBN: 979-8-89269-920-4

Printed in the United States of America

DEDICATION

To suspense, mystery readers everywhere—
you keep me writing!

CHAPTER 1

*A*s exciting as the thought of uprooting for the second time in as many years was, after taking the plunge, Decklin Kilgarry wasn't so sure. Never having lived in southern climes, cloaking humidity took a bit of getting used to. Cecily, however?

In her element.

"I never thought I could like something so much," she gushed as she and Decklin finally had time to sit in their new condo, surveying myriad boxes waiting to be unpacked.

"Well, it's different, that's for sure . . ." Then, a lackluster smile. "It sure is hot—and, it would be nice if the air conditioning worked properly."

Sensing their conversation could go belly up quickly, Cecily opted for a different topic of conversation. "When are you and Devon going to meet up?"

Good question.

As much as Decklin wanted to get his office up and running, finding reasonable rental space was turning out to be a challenge—until Devon offered to split the rent. "Look—if I'm your partner," he stated confidently, "it only makes sense I pay my share." A pause. "And, let's face it— money isn't an issue."

That was true—Devon Bryson was heir to a considerable fortune, money lining his pockets long before those controlling his inheritance were six feet under. Even so, he kept a logical head and, though he was young, there was nothing inexperienced or nouveau about him. Family money offered opportunities few have the privilege to know, yet he presented himself as one who was as regular as the next guy. "I'm hoping we can get together tomorrow," Decklin finally answered after calculating how many boxes he could unpack before passing out. "We'll have to see . . ."

"I can take care of this stuff," Cecily offered, noting the depleted expression on his face. "And, there's nothing saying we have to do it all at one time . . ." As soon as she heard her own words, she blushed at how much different she sounded than her mom. A woman to always have 'things in their place,' Cecily clearly didn't carry the same gene.

Suddenly, Decklin stood, then grabbed her hand. "C'mon—let's get something to eat. Someplace cool and air conditioned . . ."

"But . . ."

"No! I haven't taken you out to a proper place to eat in weeks, so you're due!"

Cecily grinned, loving the familiar, spontaneous spark. "Give me five . . ."

"So?" Devon glanced at his partner, beginning to think he made a huge mistake. "What do you think?"

Stunned, Decklin stared at the fully furnished office space. "It's . . . expensive!"

"I know—but, the way I figure it, if we want to make it in the Miami scene, we have to look the part." Devon paused. "And, from what I can tell from my few weeks here? We need to make an impression . . ."

Decklin scanned their new office from the doorway, wondering how he could afford his half of the monthly lease. "I don't know . . ."

"If you're worried about paying for it, don't be—our first year is already paid. And, the second . . ."

Suddenly, Decklin smiled, clapping his young partner on the shoulder. "What about the third?"

Stepping across the threshold, the impressive space was more than he could imagine. The receptionist's area a perfect distance from the door, it allowed visitors enough room to make themselves comfortable. Private offices with glass walls offered a sense of trust, presenting the impression there should never be anything to hide when it came to a successful partnership. Across the hall, a conference room including a twenty foot, handcrafted, sugar maple table accompanied by plush, black leather chairs.

"Does all of this style come from an interior designer," he asked as he admired floor-to-ceiling windows overlooking the water.

A smile. "Nope—just me. My dad happened to have a few connections, though—that's how it got done so fast." Devon took a deep breath as he, too, admired where he would spend a great deal of his time. "To be fair, however, most of it was move-in ready . . ."

Decklin shook his head. "I'm at a loss . . ." Then, a grin. "But, not for long!"

"Cool—because we have our first client."

"What?"

"I know—I didn't pass her by you first, but I have no doubt you'll agree."

"Agree about what?"

"She needs our help . . ."

Decklin was quiet for a moment, not quite sure how he felt about his partner taking the lead in their new city. The more he thought about it, however?

It didn't make a damned bit of difference.

"Tell me . . ."

Devon headed for the conference room, pulled out a chair, then presented two file folders, placing them on the table. "One for me, one for you . . ."

Again, Decklin shook his head. "I can see I need to step up my game to keep up with you!"

Devon laughed, then grabbed two waters from the small fridge tucked in the corner. "Well, I wasn't expecting a new client—but, when she asked me if we were available, how could I refuse?"

"How is it she happened to ask about private detective services?"

"Because her husband was hauled off to the clink a few days ago, and his last words before heading out of their Florida mansion door were, "Hire someone!""

"That could've meant a lawyer . . ."

"True—but, if that dude is anything like my dad, his lawyer was already on it."

Decklin smiled, thinking of how much his former student learned in such a short time. "You're right—so, what's her deal? Why was her husband arrested?"

"I don't know anything—I told her you'd be arriving in town and, as soon as you did, we'd set an appointment." Devon paused, thinking. "I imagine, however, he's already out on bail . . ."

"Why do you think so?"

"Only because she was dressed as if she stepped out of a magazine—expensive clothes, expensive style. Something with which I'm quite familiar . . ."

"Good observations—what's her name?"

"Analena Cortina—Hector is her husband."

"What do you know about either of them?" Decklin plucked his tiny spiral notepad from his shirt pocket, then reached for a pen stashed in a personalized 'Kilgarry and Bryson' cup on the conference room table. "Nice touch . . ."

"Thanks—I ordered a bunch when I arrived in Miami, figuring we'd need them sometime." Grinning, Devon, too, readied his notepad—one of the first things he learned from his mentor. "From what I read during my online research of both, they arrived in this country as immigrants, and it's no secret they're high rollers."

Decklin eyed his partner, confused about one thing. "How on earth did you happen to meet her?"

"I knew you'd ask that—at a restaurant down the street. We were standing in line and, the next thing I knew, we were having lunch—probably because the place was packed, and there weren't open tables. When one broke loose, it made sense to sit together—and, honestly, I didn't mind." As he spoke, Devon recalled the meeting, thinking the whole thing was just plain weird. "She asked me what I was doing in Miami, so I told her I was a private detective."

"Given her husband's situation, I imagine that piqued her interest . . ."

"Yep—but, when I asked her why he was arrested, she didn't want to talk about it in the restaurant. Actually, that's when I told her you'd be back in town—I didn't want to start a conversation without your being there."

Decklin nodded. "I appreciate that—so, I'm guessing you have a way to contact her. Cell would be nice . . ."

"Yep—email, too."

"Okay—give her a call! Let's see if she's serious, and what she has to say . . ." As much as Decklin would've liked a week or so to get his Florida bearings, he couldn't turn down the opportunity for a first client—especially one who dripped money.

"Now?"

"I don't see any reason to wait—do you?"

With a smile, Devon plucked his phone from his jeans pocket, then tapped the screen. A few minutes later?

Their first appointment on the books.

"Excellent," Decklin commented, the enthusiasm in his voice unmistakable. "That gives us a couple of days to prepare—and, we'll need to hustle to get our ducks in a row."

So, with their first client on the calendar, Decklin Kilgarry and Devon Bryson embarked on a new life—one poised to lure them down roads never imagined. Of course, neither suspected that may be the case, though Decklin had the experience to know better. Devon, however, had no idea what may be on the horizon for him and his partner.

No idea, at all.

To those who were interested, Hector Cortina was the epitome of a self-made man. Brought to the States by his parents when he was twelve, it didn't take him long to branch out personally and professionally. Friends were easily acquired and, as he watched and learned from his father, it became clear he didn't want the same difficult life. No—if Hector had anything to do with it, he'd rise to the top before the age of twenty.

He did, too.

Though his early years weren't particularly admirable, Hector's teenage entrepreneurial efforts awarded him with a means of attending college, medical school, and setting up his own office by the time he was thirty-five. Was he taking advantage of those who deemed they were, somehow, not enough? Of course, but wasn't that what a plastic surgeon was known to do?

During his youth, how Hector obtained funds to achieve such heights were always kept private, his parents also preferring not to know. To them, as long as he made his own way, how he made his money really didn't matter—and, though they were close, they allowed him space to live his own life. Parenting skills weren't a concern as long as dear Hector made enough money to throw into the family pot.

And, he made plenty.

So, by the time he opened his first plastic surgery office in South Beach, he had everything he needed for a successful practice. New clients proved to be no problem and, before he could spit, he was rolling in enough moolah to make his family proud. Purchasing a palatial estate for them was quite a reward for their not interfering in his life when he was a mere boy, one which he was more than pleased to give. By the time he reached his mid-forties?

A booming medical practice, a wife, and two wonderful children.

It was unfortunate, however, he chose to mirror his own upbringing by allowing his boys to manage their own lives— something his wife abhorred. But, that being the case, when they reached the tender age of fifteen, she, too, decided her life would be easier by allowing them freedom from being tethered to her or their father. A mistake?

Probably.

Of course, none of that was up for discussion when Analena Cortina met with Decklin and Devon—all she needed was someone to get to the bottom of what she considered her husband's misguided arrest. How to go about such a thing, though, was a foreign thought—so, when she serendipitously ran into Devon Bryson a few days prior, there was little doubt it was her lucky day.

"Mrs. Cortina? I'm Decklin Kilgarry—it's a pleasure to meet you." Decklin extended his hand, a gesture she promptly refused. "And, you've already met Devon . . ."

"Yes . . ."

Although it's difficult to keep first impressions at bay, Decklin immediately recognized the pitfalls of new money. Dressed as if she stepped out of a top designer's studio, Analena presented herself as one of the socially elite, easily bothered by those who didn't measure up to expectations. "I appreciate your seeing me . . ."

And, that was all she had to offer as Decklin led her to the conference room, Devon following as he took note of everything about her. His initial impression?

Not the same woman he met in the restaurant.

Soon situated in the conference room, Decklin casually sat back in his chair as if he were in his best friend's home. "So," he began with a smile, "why are you here?"

Analena smiled briefly as she extracted a tissue from her designer handbag, then glanced at Devon. "My husband was arrested . . ."

"For?"

Silence.

A sure sign of embarrassment.

"I understand," Decklin continued, "how difficult discussing personal issues can be, Mrs. Cortina—but, if we're to help, I need to understand everything."

"I know . . ." Suddenly, Analena straightened slightly, dabbed at her nose once or twice, then focused on Decklin. "I don't know why my husband was arrested, and he didn't tell me—but, I believe someone is to blame."

An interesting tidbit—a husband not telling his wife why he was hauled in for quality time in the Miami jail? Odd, if not a reason for concern. "To blame? You mean you think someone set him up," Decklin asked as he jotted a few notes.

Another dab.

"Yes—and, that is why I come to you." As she spoke, her native accent became more pronounced, a signal of emotional angst. "But, whatever the reason, I know my husband did not do it!"

"Okay—that gives me something to go on. But, in order for Devon and I to do our best for you, we need to understand your husband—so, why do you think someone set him up?"

"Because my husband is a law-abiding man! He's kind and caring—he would never be involved with anything that could make him be arrested! Ever!"

"Who do you think set him up?"

Again, silence.

It was then the atmosphere in the room changed, becoming heavy and unpleasant. "I think you know, Mrs. Cortina . . ." He watched Analena bow her head as if in prayer. "Again, if we're to do our best work for you, it's important we know everything—and, of course, what you say doesn't leave this room."

Slowly, Analena raised her head, her eyes dark with intention. "Her name is Gisele . . ."

"Last name?"

"Escalante."

As Decklin jotted down the name, Devon picked up the thread. "Why do you think Gisele Escalante has something to do with your husband's arrest?"

"Because it is what she does!"

Devon glanced at Decklin, hoping he would take the lead, yet knowing he wouldn't. "And, what is it she does?"

"Santeria."

Decklin's turn. "I'm afraid I don't understand—what is Santeria?"

"A religion of our culture—it is dark, Mr. Kilgarry, yet strong."

Silence descended as Decklin and Devon listened, both suddenly uneasy. "What are you trying to say, Analena," Decklin finally asked.

"Gisele Escalante is the same as darkness, and she threw a curse on my husband. One designed to destroy him. His soul. I know it . . ."

Devon shifted uncomfortably in his chair, beginning to wonder if he made a mistake that day in the restaurant. "Please explain . . ."

So, for the next hour, Analena Cortina spilled her guts, telling her newly contracted private detectives everything—well, as much as she knew. What Decklin realized?

A tip of the iceberg thing.

CHAPTER 2

Cecily shoved a few boxes out of the way, then handed Decklin a plastic cup. "Perhaps not the classiest thing," she laughed, "but, it'll do the job! And, no, it's not wine—it's iced tea to take the heat off."

"Even better!" With his customary smile and a peck, Decklin cleared a place on the couch, then plopped down to cool off. "Why didn't you tell me it's so hot here," he chided as he took a sip.

"It's Florida, Deck. It should come as no surprise—and, the air conditioning guy is coming at the end of the week." Armed with her own cup, Cecily joined him, eager to hear about his day. "So, how did your meeting with the new client go?"

"Interesting—and, I think she scared the crap out of Devon!"

"Scared him? What do you mean?"

Propping his feet up on a box, Decklin made himself comfortable, ready to tell all. "Well, she's a rather strange woman . . ."

"In what way?"

Decklin thought for a moment before explaining his first impression. There was little doubt Analena Cortina hailed from big money, and was part of the socially elite scene—which was great from the standpoint of being paid. She offered a hefty retainer to bring Devon and him on board, obviously making them feel more confident in their client. "I don't know exactly—but, when she began to explain why she was there, it was weird."

"How so?"

"Well, the atmosphere in the room changed—as if a wet blanket descended upon it." As the words came out of Decklin's mouth, he couldn't help thinking of what Analena Cortina said. "She thinks someone cursed her husband . . ."

"What?"

"I know—that's why I think she scared the crap out of Devon. He didn't know what to think . . ."

Cecily was quiet for a moment, having no idea what Analena meant. "She actually thinks someone threw a curse on her husband?"

"I think so—she mentioned Santeria."

Suddenly, Cecily's face blanched. "Santeria? Are you sure?"

"Yep—that's what she said." Glancing at her, Decklin recognized something was out of sync. "Why?"

Placing her cup on a cardboard box, Cecily hesitated, wondering how much she wanted to disclose about her culture. "Do you know what Santeria is?"

"No—it's the first thing I'm going to research, though. Unless you can tell me everything I need to know . . ."

A smile. "How much time do you have?"

Well, that wasn't good.

Decklin shifted uncomfortably, noticing a distinct change in his better half. "I don't like the sound of that . . ."

"And, you shouldn't—Santeria is a dark, Cuban religion, although many practitioners don't see it that way. It made its way to America when immigrants arrived here—especially Florida."

As much as Decklin wanted to take notes, he didn't dare—it didn't take a genius to realize the topic of discussion was one of memories for Cecily.

It took experience.

"How do you know so much about it?"

"Because my heritage is one of voodoo and Santeria—and, I know more about it than I care to." Cecily turned to him, a single tear tracing her cheek. "There's so much you don't know . . ."

Instinctively, Decklin pulled her to him, holding her close. "Obviously, it's something that upsets you—but, I'm here to help you through it."

Sadly, the moment didn't last long.

Cecily pulled back, leveling her most serious look. "If someone knowledgeable about Santeria is truly responsible for throwing a curse on your client's husband, you must be very careful. Devon, too . . ."

"Oh, I don't think . . ."

Suddenly, Cecily stood, her eyes flashing. "You don't know the damage such a thing can do!" With that, she headed up the stairs to their bedroom, slamming the door.

Stunned, Decklin watched her go, wondering what the hell just happened. Obviously, he pressed a button without knowing it, her reaction one he never suspected. *What was that about*, he wondered, immediately understanding the first thing he needed to do. It wasn't an apology to Cecily for bringing up something he didn't understand—it was research laying claim to his time.

As he listened to water turn on in the upstairs shower, he fired up his laptop, entering 'Santeria' in the search box. What he learned?

No wonder Cecily was upset.

Hector Cortina glared at his wife, anger flashing. "She will not get away with this," he promised, his voice rising to a level Analena didn't like—or, accept. Although she understood his frustration, she also understood it was exactly what Gisele Escalante wanted.

It was how she could win.

"Well, tonight isn't the night to discuss it—we have our Social Hour."

"Tonight?"

"Yes! Tonight!" Analena turned again to her vanity mirror, making sure her husband's work was looking its best. "You know it's every Friday," she commented as she relocated a wayward strand of hair.

Hector said nothing, knowing how important it was to keep up appearances—and, in Analena's book, it was what kept her going. With the boys growing away from her, there was really little to her life except charity work, as well as making sure she remained in Miami's social scene. "So, for the next couple of hours," she continued, "I suggest you forget about Gisele Escalante . . ."

"Forget? She's trying to destroy me! How in the hell can I forget such a thing?" Of course, neither Hector nor Analena knew for certain if Gisele Escalante were at the center of Hector's being arrested—but, to them, it made sense.

Slowly, Analena rose from her vanity stool, then joined him on the edge of the bed. "Your day will come, my darling—all in good time."

Well, if ever there were a cryptic conversation, that was probably it. "What the hell does that mean?"

A smile. "Only what you and I have known for a very long time . . ."

"And, that is?"

Analena laughed softly, then patted her husband's hand. "It's better to get even . . ." With that, she grabbed her lightweight, designer shawl from the corner of the bed. "And, as you recall, we happen to be quite good at it . . ."

"So, after a night to think on it, what do you think of our new client," Decklin asked as he met with Devon in their new office the following morning. "Interesting, yes?"

"You can say that—but, I don't mind telling you when we met with her?" Devon focused on the table as if thinking of something important. Serious. "She was different when we were at the restaurant . . ."

Decklin nodded. "That's doesn't surprise me—I admit there's something unsettling about her. Even so, we committed to . . ."

"That's just it," Devon interrupted. "What are we committed to? Analena doesn't know why Hector was arrested, yet she seems to think someone placed a curse on him. So, what does she need us for?" As Devon spoke, there was little doubt he was upset.

"Are you sorry we took the case," Decklin asked, trying to get a handle on why his partner was questioning their decision to work with Analena Cortina.

"Hell, no! But, I admit I don't like the sound of witchcraft stuff—if, in fact, that's what it is."

Decklin was silent, recalling his conversation with Cecily the evening prior as well as his research. "I don't blame you. But, remember—it's only Analena's suspicion, and there may be something completely different at work."

"Such as?"

"Good question—isn't that why we're sitting here in our lovely new offices, trying to figure it out?" A pause as Decklin let his question sink in. "So, are you in?"

"Of course, I'm in—I'm sure as hell not going to let you go out there on your own without knowing what you're dealing with!"

"I appreciate that—so, let's get to work." Another pause as Decklin tried to assess what they already knew. "Did you happen to research Santeria?"

"Yep—and, what I read, I didn't like."

"Agreed—when I told Cec about it, she didn't think too much of our new case, either."

"Did she say why?"

"Not really—but, she seems to have a working knowledge of Santeria. Last night, however, wasn't the time to dive into it more . . ."

Nothing more needed to be said—though Devon was a young pup compared to his partner, he knew things left unsaid were the way of the wise.

"So, how about if we forget the Santeria thing for a minute," Decklin suggested. "With that out of the way, who would be most interested in Hector Cortina's business?"

"A dissatisfied patient?"

"Exactly what I'm thinking—as dramatic as the whole Santeria thing sounds, I think we're looking at something far more in keeping with reality." Decklin paused, glancing at the notes he compiled after they spoke with Analena. "Maybe, someone threw Hector Cortina under the bus . . ."

Devon said nothing, digesting Decklin's possible theory. "But, if that's the case, the question is why? A pause. "The first thing I can think of is Hector screwed someone over . . ."

A nod. "You might be right—so, when we look at the type of people Analena and Hector are, at least on the surface, what do we see?"

"Well, there's little doubt they like money and, from what Analena told us, her husband is a highly respected plastic surgeon . . ." Devon, too, jotted down a few notes, then focused again on Decklin. "Research confirms . . ."

"Correct. So, why would the cops pick up someone of Hector's stature?"

Devon shook his head slightly, realizing his fear of something—Santeria—didn't hold water. "I got nothin' . . ."

"Okay—when thinking about it, what's the one thing that could piss someone off in Hector's line of business?"

"A botched plastic surgery . . ."

"Right again," Decklin praised with a grin.

"But, how do we know who he worked on? He sure as hell isn't going to turn over his client list . . ." Devon, tossed his pen on the table, then locked his hands behind his head.

"Maybe—maybe not. While he may not be for turning over information like that to us, Analena may very well be willing to give us a list."

"All she can say is no," Devon agreed. "But, I wonder—if Hector doesn't want to divulge his clients to us, perhaps there's a reason other than patient confidentiality."

"Maybe—but, first on our list of things to do?"

A silent response.

"Schedule a meeting with Hector Cortina . . ."

A few weeks into becoming comfortable in his new hometown, Decklin realized one thing—money was revered above all else. So, it was easy to recognize the lifestyle Analena and her husband led—Social Hours every Friday, precisely at seven, those attending known to be part of the best circles. If one should miss such a soirée?

Talked about for weeks behind backs that no longer mattered.

So, when Analena and Hector showed up as if they hadn't a care in the world, no one was the wiser Hector had legal problems beyond his control. Laughing and chatting as they always did on Friday nights, no one paid attention to Hector's glancing at the door every five seconds, or his attempt to ascertain if anyone in the room had anything to do with his current issues. If they did?

A topic of conversation for later.

Analena, however, was more in her element, caring little about her husband's legal issues—though, perhaps she should've. The truth was if his ship went down, so would hers, and her lifestyle would be in the toilet—something worth considering should the prospect of prison time come knocking at their door.

Then again, in her mind, all of it was nothing but conjecture, and she was certain Hector could rectify the situation. If not?

'Rectifying' would turn to her.

CHAPTER 3

As it turned out, Analena was more than happy to provide a list of her husband's clients—with reassurance, of course, said list would remain under lock and key until the time it was no longer needed. After that?

A date with a match.

"No wonder this guy is rich," Devon commented as he flipped through several pages of names.

Decklin laughed as he looked through his own copy. "And, it makes me wonder if cosmetic surgery patients go to the surgeon more than once. I'm guessing they do—

if not, however, that accounts for the long list of names." For the first time in a while, Decklin felt like a newbie in the detective biz—he knew nothing about plastic surgery, cosmetic surgery, or anything else that had to do with altering one's body. "I think we need to have a plant . . ."

"What do you mean?"

"You know—someone who pretends to be someone they're not."

"You mean schedule a bogus appointment with Hector?"

Decklin nodded, then smiled. "Exactly. And, I think I know just the person . . ."

It was then Devon laughed, picking up his pen from the conference table. "Do you think she'll do it?"

"Well, I don't know—but, it doesn't hurt to ask!"

"You want me to do what?" Cecily stared at Decklin, a kitchen knife poised in her hand.

"You might want to put that down," Decklin teased, knowing he was going to need to explain his request for her acting services. Waiting as she placed the knife on the counter and turned to him with arms crossed, he figured what he had to say might not be an easy sell. "I need your help . . ."

"With your Santeria case?"

"Well, yes—but, we're not following the Santeria angle. At least for now . . ."

Wiping her hands on a dish towel, Cecily joined him at the kitchen table. "That's good because I don't want any part of it—so, what can I do to help?"

A long pause as Decklin gathered his words. "We really need you to infiltrate Hector Cortina's practice . . ."

"Infiltrate?"

"Well, maybe the wrong word—although, when I think about it, it's not a bad idea. But, we can talk about that later—what Devon and I need from you now is to pretend you're looking for a bit of sprucing up."

Cecily's eyes narrowed as she got the gist of his suggestion. "You mean you want me to pretend I'm looking for plastic surgery?"

A nod. "Yes—but, nothing big. Maybe a nose job . . . or, something."

"You're serious . . ."

Decklin was quiet, well aware their conversation wasn't going as planned. "All you have to do is go to a consultation appointment—nothing else." Decklin hesitated for a second, knowing she needed to hear something else. "And, I'm certainly not suggesting you need plastic surgery . . ."

"You better not be!"

Then, a smile. "So—will you do it?"

"Maybe—what do I get from the deal?" Cecily sat back, refusing to take her eyes from his. "Well?"

"I'll think of something . . ."

Within the week, an appointment was on the books and, when the day arrived, Cecily Robinson stepped across the threshold of Hector's office door into pure luxury. *Holy shit*, she thought as she approached the receptionist to check in. *This guy's into serious bucks . . .*

And, so it seemed to be.

Escorted to Hector Cortina's evaluation room promptly at her appointment time, Cecily carefully eyed everything as she passed. Expensive, rose gold picture frames graced the hallway walls, the paintings created by names she recognized. The evaluation room was the same with diplomas front and center, all perfectly placed, certain to capture a patient's eye while subliminally convincing them of Dr. Cortina's credentials and qualifications.

By five minutes after the hour, Cecily was in the wings awaiting her performance.

"Ms. Robinson?" Hand out for the customary shake. "I'm Dr. Cortina . . ."

Taking her cue, Cecily accepted the gesture, then settled down to business and, after a bit of small talk, it was time to get to the reason she was there. "As you can see, I'm not a spring chicken," she began, "and, I think I could use with a little sprucing up!"

Decklin's words—not hers.

"What exactly do you have in mind?" Dr. Cortina's eye's scanned her body with nothing but medical interest. "You look healthy and, from what I can see, you're aging gracefully—so, what type of sprucing up do you think is necessary?"

"Lips, and maybe my nose . . ." From her first few weeks in South Beach, it was apparent duck lips were a beauty requisite. "I've always thought my lips were thin . . ." A lie?

Of course.

But, it was one Dr. Hector Cortina believed and, soon, he was engrossed in discussing possibilities. Thirty minutes later?

Cecily opened the office building's door, stepping into a sweltering heat, not thrilled with the fact the good doctor pointed out more things needing attention in addition to a lip and nose job. A part of his game?

Probably.

Watching her husband in the mirror, Amelia Sandoval plucked off her earrings, placing them carefully in their box. "You didn't notice," she asked, keeping an eye on him as he stripped off his tie.

"Notice what?"

"Hector—at the Social Hour! I pointed it out to you last week when we saw him!"

"And, just what is it you're pointing out, my dear?" Thomas Sandoval turned to her as he fiddled with his French cuffs, placing the cufflinks on his nightstand. "If you're asking me if I noticed anything different about Hector, the answer is no."

"No? Seriously, Thomas?" Amelia suddenly turned, as if ready to confront her worst enemy. "I can't believe you haven't noticed!"

"Then, I ask again—what exactly are you talking about?"

"Well, the first thing is I swear to God he's lost twenty pounds in the last week—and, he's pale."

Thomas Sandoval smiled, well aware his wife was likely making something from nothing. "To answer your question, then, I did notice he lost a bit of weight—but, I don't think it's a concern."

"What about his not looking healthy?"

"You mean his being pale?" Finally ready to call it a night, Thomas crawled into bed, pulling the satin top sheet and light blanket up to his chin, carefully folding them over his chest.

"Yes!" Amelia paused, recalling the previous two Social Hours. "I think something's going on with him . . ."

As much as Thomas loved his wife, from the time they met, he couldn't understand her proclivity for jumping to conclusions. It was one of the things that drove him nuts, but, being the dutiful husband he was, it was best to never mention obvious shortcomings. "Even if there is, my dear, it's none of our business . . ." Then, he patted the empty space beside him. "Come to bed—it's late."

"In a few minutes . . ." With that, she made sure everything in her closet was as it should be, closing the door behind her as she crossed to their bedroom door. "Don't wait up . . ."

It was a directive he often heard, choosing to not argue for he knew minutes would turn into an hour—possibly more. "Your altar?"

"Of course—there are things I must know."

Without looking at him, she closed the bedroom door gently, looking forward to time by herself. Since the time they married over a decade prior, her religion was one thing she chose to hold close. Having grown up with beliefs many preferred not to discuss, there was little doubt she felt the need for personal privacy.

Her feet slightly chilled on the veined marble floor, Amelia descended the stairs, making certain her two boys were nowhere to be seen—the last thing she needed was having to explain something that was none of their business. Moments later, she withdrew a key from her silk dressing gown pocket, then slipped it into the lock, turning it carefully.

Stepping into the dark room, Amelia closed the door behind her then crossed to a small altar where she lit several candles—just enough to illuminate the cypress wood tabletop that had been in her family for generations. Then, with three small bowls flanking three partially-burned candles, she laid a fresh cigar horizontally in front of them. *Everything is perfect,* she thought as she prepared herself for the ritual she knew so well.

As candles flickered, she pulled out a small stool then sat, resting her palms gently on the surface of the smooth wood. Then, again reaching into her robe pocket, she pulled out a small, sepia-colored photograph, resting it against a plain, black urn.

With candle flames mirrored in her eyes, Amelia lit the cigar with one of the candles, blowing its thick, acrid smoke at the photo—and, it was then she spoke, her words unintelligible. Chanting her desires, she gently picked up the photograph, raising it to her God.

And, there she stayed until it was done . . .

Two days later?

Hector Cortina was unceremoniously hauled out of his posh offices in handcuffs for the second time in as many weeks. Of course, when the media got ahold of it, videos were plentiful, begging the question who tipped them off? "They had to have known," Decklin commented as he and Devon watched the news on the large television in their conference room.

"Which means," Devon proposed, "this is bigger than we thought . . ." He glanced at Decklin, then returned his attention to the T.V. "My gut tells me Hector Cortina is involved in something that can put him away for years."

It was a possibility, too—the fact the Feds were suddenly involved made it obvious Hector's crime was far beyond that of local authorities. "We need to speak with Analena as soon as possible," Decklin advised as he jotted down a few notes. "Do you want to do the honors?"

"You mean call her now?"

"No time like the present . . ."

Unfortunately, it was a call that didn't go particularly well. As one might expect, due to Hector's unanticipated incarceration, Analena Cortina was a total wreck, jabbering a mile a minute as she tried to explain what happened. "I understand," Devon appeased, "but, I think it's wise if we meet this afternoon to discuss what changed with your husband's circumstances . . ."

"No—not today!" Morphing into a full-blown rant, Analena's voice pitched higher, causing Devon to hold the phone away from his ear. Glancing at Decklin, he pointed to a time on their calendar for the next day, eventually cementing it with their client.

So, with a proposed meeting solidified, all Decklin and Devon could do was speculate when it came to the plastic surgeon's legal woes—yet, both knew speculation didn't mean jack shit. Until Analena Cortina was sitting across from them?

They knew nothing.

CHAPTER 4

*B*y coffee time the following morning, there wasn't a soul in the state who didn't know about the illustrious cosmetic surgeon's impromptu visit to the nearest slammer. Even though little information was available by trusted news sources, there was enough to set tongues a waggin' and, by noon, it seemed everyone had an opinion regarding Hector Cortina's legal transgressions—whatever they were.

Including Gisele Escalante.

Not that Hector's situation came as a surprise—it was, in fact, quite the opposite. *Finally meeting your fate*, she asked silently as she read the latest article about his arrest

on her cell. In her mind, Hector was getting everything he
deserved and, hopefully, more. Having known him since
he was a mere boy, there wasn't anything she liked about
him, and nothing changed over the years. No—to her way
of thinking, he was nothing more than a common criminal,
gleefully taking hard-earned money from those who thought
poorly of themselves. Although, to be fair, why shouldn't
he? After all, his chosen profession was geared to aiding his
patients toward self-respect, something most lacked when
pulling on his office door.

Even so, Gisele was well aware Hector harbored nothing
but greed, giving little consideration to his clientele's well-
being. If a patient looked better six weeks after going under
the knife? A job well done.

A bank account well-bolstered.

Unfortunately, Hector's acceptable facial reinventions
were becoming fewer, and those not satisfied with their
new reflection in the mirror were becoming more vocal.
Until his arrest, however, he somehow managed to keep
his dwindling reputation at bay, shielding his family from
patients' dissatisfaction. According to him, there was no
reason for concern, thereby allowing Analena and the two
boys free reign when it came to spending. So much so, in
fact, when creditors came calling at his office, there was
little left with which to pay.

So, when Gisele Escalante learned of Hector's arrest?

Just desserts.

Though Decklin and Devon didn't know it when they accepted Analena Cortina as their first client, her propensity for being tardy was on full display when she arrived for her second appointment nearly an hour late—something that was just fine with her.

But, it wasn't fine with Decklin.

Noting the missing apology, he led her to the conference room where Devon was opening bottles of water, placing them on the table. Waiting until they were seated and comfortable, it was then Decklin asked his first question. "Why was your husband arrested again, Analena?"

"I don't . . ."

"You don't know?" A pause as he considered which course to take. "I'm afraid I find that difficult to believe . . ."

Perhaps not the best approach, but the fact she was late and disrespectful of their time was still sticking in his craw. "Are you calling me a liar," she asked, as if Decklin's answer would convince her to stay or go.

"Of course not—I merely meant there has to be a good explanation for why you don't know the reasons Hector was arrested." A smile. "Please, sit—I meant no offense."

Somewhat appeased, Analena took her seat, then snatched a tissue from her tiny Gucci handbag. "My husband never discusses business with me—or, anyone in our family. He only says it is our job to enjoy the rewards . . ."

"The rewards from his working?"

A nod.

Her response making sense, Decklin instantly understood the situation—Hector Cortina was a man of secrets. "I understand—so, please tell us everything you know." A brief glance at Devon who was taking notes. "When did you learn Hector was arrested—before or after the authorities visited his office?"

"After he was arrested—he told me to call his lawyer."

"Did you?"

Another nod. "Immediately—and, he said he would head straight to the police."

"You mean where Hector was being detained?"

"Yes." Analena focused on the floor for a moment or two before delicately dabbing her eyes with the tissue, careful not to disturb her eye makeup.

"Who's Hector's lawyer," Devon suddenly asked, his pen poised while waiting for an answer.

Analena hesitated, uncertain if she should divulge such information. "We have to know everything," Decklin gently prompted, "if we're to help you." And, that was true—he and Devon still had nothing to go on, leaving their investigation at the starting line.

A dab and a nod, yet still no answer.

"Okay, then let's begin with the list of your husband's patients—is there anyone on it who gives you cause for concern?"

"I don't remember the names—I didn't look at them before I met with you."

Instantly, Devon jumped up, taking the list of the names to the copier, returning moments later. "Here you go—we can go over them together."

Decklin stifled a smile as he noticed Analena's somewhat shocked expression. "Excellent—thank you, Devon." A silent moment as Analena hesitatingly drew the list to her with her fingertips, as if its contents may be reason for personal downfall. "How about if we begin at the top—and, I'll appreciate your providing as much information as you can about each one."

So, for the next hour, there they sat, Analena professing to know only a few of her husband's patients—something Decklin and Devon knew was a bunch of crap. "She's definitely hiding something," Devon commented as their client closed the office door behind her.

"Agreed—and, I found it interesting as we made our way down the list, she became more agitated."

"I noticed the same thing—it's as if she were pissed at her husband for making her endure such an intense grilling!"

Decklin chuckled, noting the sarcasm. "I've been waiting to get a glimpse of who she really is—and, I get the sense she really has no personal identity of her own."

"Meaning?"

"She looks manufactured—and, her personality feels the same."

Devon said nothing, trying to understand what his partner was telling him. "You mean she's what her husband wants her to be?"

A nod. "It's what he demands . . ."

By the end of his second day in the local slammer, Hector Cortina waltzed into his palatial home as if nothing happened, hugging his children while giving his wife an obligatory peck on the cheek. Looking no worse for the wear, it was a bit of surprise when he arrived dressed in a designer suit—certainly not the attire one usually expects when returning home from the slammer. Still, no one appeared to notice and, after an hour or two and a good meal, things seemed back to normal.

But, they weren't back to normal.

Although Hector had stories to tell, it was clear he chose to share none of them with his family. Protecting them? Maybe. Or, perhaps, remaining mum was easier— no explanation meant no questions. Besides, his attorney advised him to shut the hell up about anything and everything, reinforcing the fact the more Hector blabbed, the more authorities were willing to investigate.

Sage advice.

However, refusing to speak of his recent experience wasn't Hector's style, so, when the next Social Hour rolled around, he was more than willing to confide a portion of his troubles to those in his private circle—you know, a choice one or two whom he thought he could trust. "But, they can't keep me from what I do best," he bragged as the tiny group of listeners inched away for no other reason than they didn't want to be involved. If, in fact, there were truth to swirling allegations—which were, of course, under wraps at least for a while—it was significantly easier to move to the fringes of Hector's life rather than engage.

Had he thought about his situation, he may have recognized the purpose of their Social Hour—gossip in its most valuable and purest form. Most times, what circulated among Social Hour members was nothing more than titillating fluff—but, every once in a while, something arose with a little more tooth to it. A bit more chew. So, when Hector's mug shot was plastered all over the Internet as well as the local news, it was nothing less than a gift from God.

After all, gossip was what the Social Hour did best.

"Let's divvy up surveillance," Decklin suggested as he and Devon agreed on a plan to gather information regarding Hector Cortina. "Who do you prefer to tail—Hector or Analena?"

Devon grinned, knowing both would be difficult simply because neither he nor Decklin knew the area as well as they should. "Either . . ."

"Okay—I'll take Hector while you tail Analena. I can't help thinking Hector is going to be spending a lot of time with his lawyer, and I want to see whom else he meets."

A nod. "Works for me—let's check in every couple of hours," Devon suggested, feeling doing so would make him a little more comfortable with his assignment.

"Agreed—do what you did for the Greyson Garfield case, and you'll be fine."

So, with that, they parted, each devoting the day to gathering information—and, for the first few hours, there was little to report. Early in the afternoon, however?

Hector Cortina met up with a sweet little number at least fifteen years his junior who was decked out in a short skirt and ripped designer tank top. *Family or friend*, Decklin wondered as he watched Hector open the passenger's door of his black sedan, gently placing a hand at the small of the young woman's back.

Decklin kept an eye on the car as Hector pulled into traffic moments later, trailing several cars behind even though there was little chance of Hector's spotting him— especially since he'd never met the private detective his wife hired. *Something that's about to change*, Decklin thought as he followed, knowing it was time to meet the man who was paying his fee.

Within fifteen, Hector turned onto a side street, one away from the city's hustle, minutes later parking in front of a nondescript, out-of-the way local restaurant. Keeping his eyes trained on the unlikely couple as they entered, it was then Decklin had a decision to make. Since Hector hadn't met him, it seemed a golden opportunity to observe the doctor in his native habitat—one Decklin couldn't refuse.

Figuring Hector and the young woman were enjoying a forbidden tryst, Decklin waited for several minutes before entering what he would soon learn was a small, family-owned business. As he stepped across the threshold, there was little doubt the establishment had been serving locals of South Beach for decades. A hostess stand sporting chipped paint stood inside the door, the dining room offering an impression most diners probably wouldn't enjoy. What they would enjoy?

The wafting fragrance of homemade Italian.

With a few minutes to check out the menu prior to being seated, the restaurant's history was front and center, complete with photos of past generations. Once touted as South Beach's finest Italian eatery, its current disrepair left a more dubious impression, prompting Decklin to wonder if it made its money by something other than delicious food.

"Welcome to Rossi's," a voice suddenly greeted as he reviewed the menu. "Where would you like to sit?"

"Well," Decklin replied as he scanned the dining room, "how about that booth by the window?" Then, a smile. "This is my first time here, so I'm going to rely on you to tell me what's good!" As the server led him to his seat, he glanced at the table where Hector and the young woman sat, chatting and smiling as if they'd know each other for years, and one thing was clear—the young woman wasn't family or a friend.

So, for the next hour, Decklin nursed his plate of homemade lasagna followed by mouth-watering tiramisu, all the while keeping an eye on the two lovebirds—until his cell buzzed, notifying him of a text from Devon.

Surveillance in progress—interesting!
Meet at the office at 3?

With a final glance at Hector and his lunch date, Decklin tossed a generous tip on the table, thanking his server on his way out. "I'll be back," he promised with an engaging smile as he glanced at his watch.

"How about tomorrow," the hostess asked with a grin as she glanced at the table, noticing his tip was more than generous.

Smiling, Decklin stepped into the sunlight, several black sedans and SUVs parked in front of the restaurant catching his eye—yet, the dining room was nearly empty. Odd? Yes. Concerning?

Maybe.

CHAPTER 5

By the time Decklin returned to his office, Devon had already arrived, fresh coffee brewing in their small kitchen. "You're a good man," Decklin grinned as he prepared his coffee mug by adding packaged cream. "Although, after my lunch, I'm not sure if I can put another thing in my stomach!"

"Good food?"

"Probably the best Italian food I've had . . ."

So, within minutes, both settled in Decklin's office, each ready to share results of their individual surveillances. "Okay," Devon began, "for the most part, tailing Analena yielded nothing—except when she met someone for lunch at a ritzy restaurant on Miami's Ocean Drive."

"Do you know who?"

Devon grinned, taking a sip of his coffee. "Surely, you don't doubt my ability . . ." Another grin. "Amelia Sandoval."

"You recognized her?"

"No—I managed to con it out of the restaurant hostess. I went inside after they left, and struck up a conversation with her."

Taking note of his partner's high-end attire, Decklin imagined Devon had no problem convincing the hostess to reveal a name. "Well done!"

"And, I got a date out of it . . ."

"Seriously?"

"Yep—I figure it might be handy to know who frequents the restaurant, and who better to know the comings and goings other than the hostess?" A pause. "And, she was cute, too . . ."

Decklin leaned back in his chair, resting his coffee mug on its arm as he held it. "Good thinking—so, tell me about Analena and . . ."

"Amelia Sandoval."

"Right—what did you notice?"

"Well," Devon replied as he flipped through a few pages of his spiral notepad, "what stood out is they were very comfortable with each other which, in my book, rules out meeting for the first time."

"Tell me . . ."

"When Analena left the restaurant with Amelia, they were laughing—and, I got the feeling they'd known each other for a long time. I may be wrong, but . . ."

Decklin shook his head as he jotted a few notes. "No—in our line of business, going with your gut has merit. You're probably right—if they just met, I doubt they'd come across as good friends." He paused as he wrote down a few questions. "So—what do you make of it?"

"At first, nothing—but, I did a quick search on Amelia Sandoval after I got back here, and it turns out she's the wife of a cosmetic surgeon in Miami."

"Interesting—what else did you learn?" Decklin stopped writing, focusing on his partner. "You look like the Cheshire cat . . ."

Another sip. "Well, now that you mention it . . ." Devon passed a manila folder across Decklin's desk. "There was one juicy tidbit—it seems Amelia Sandoval was caught in a what was described as a 'tawdry' affair a few years ago." A pause. "And, nobody would've known about it had it not been for early-on social gossip . . ."

"How do you know?"

Devon blushed slightly as if caught with his hand in the cookie jar. "I don't, really—but, I know money, and I know the elite's desire to hold on to it. Silencing gossip costs big bucks . . ."

"So, what does that have to do with our case?"

"Well, after a detailed Internet search, the gossip about Amelia Sandoval hit the skids and, after a couple of weeks, nothing more was written about it or said publicly. At least as far as I know . . ."

Decklin was quiet for a few seconds, weighing what Devon told him. "Okay—you're saying someone paid hush money to keep word of the affair out of the press."

"Exactly."

Again, Decklin was quiet before asking his next question. "I suppose it's too much to ask with whom Amelia Sandoval had a spicy tryst . . ."

"Not really—it was none other than Hector Cortina."

Decklin said nothing as a familiar excitement began to take root. "Well, now—that leaves us with a bunch of questions, doesn't it?"

A nod. "So, as of now, we have four players—Analena and Hector, as well as Amelia and her husband."

"Her husband?"

"Well, yeah. If her husband is a colleague of Hector Cortina, it makes sense . . ."

"Or, competitor . . ." Decklin interrupted. "Either way, it stands to reason he wouldn't be too pleased about the local media's attention on something so displeasing." Then, a broad smile. "Excellent work! Now, are you ready to hear what I did with my afternoon other than stuff my face with lasagna?"

Devon laughed, then headed for the coffee pot. "Yep! I can't wait . . ."

"You're home!" Cecily dropped her purse on the foyer table, then plopped into their most comfy chair. "What a day!"

Decklin smiled, then stood behind her, gently massaging her neck and shoulders. "Care to share?"

"Oh, God—I hate that phrase!"

"Okay—I'll rephrase. What the hell happened to have you in such a mood?"

Not exactly what Cecily was expecting. "A mood?" She turned and glared at him, shrugging away from his touch. Then, kicking off her sandals, she grabbed them with one hand and headed up the stairs, leaving her better half to wonder what the hell he said that was so wrong. It was true— she was in a mood, although 'a snit' may be more descriptive, and, it was becoming a regular thing during recent weeks. "I didn't mean . . ." he called as he watched her feet vanish after landing on the top step.

Nothing.

Knowing Cecily wouldn't reappear anytime soon, Decklin grabbed a beer from the fridge, then parked in his favorite chair, trying to figure out what was bothering her. *I can solve bloody murders,* he thought as he took a long draw, *but I can't figure out what's eating the one person I love . . .*

And, that pissed him off.

Thomas Sandoval glanced at the clock on his nightstand, then checked his tie in the mirror, straightening it slightly. The one thing he despised about the Friday evening Social Hour was the unspoken requirement of wearing a tie. Still, he understood—when reaching a certain pinnacle in life, it was critical to telegraph his good fortune and success. After all, isn't envy life's best motivator?

Of course, it is.

As his wife's reflection appeared behind him, he turned, roving her body with a critical eye. "That's what you're wearing," he asked, a frown forming on his otherwise uncreased brow.

"What's wrong with this? It cost a fortune!"

"Turn," he demanded. "So I can get the full effect . . ."

Embarrassment flooding every vein, Amelia obliged, knowing he would have something to say.

He did.

"You're beginning to look a little . . . plump, my dear." A prolonged pause as he assessed what needed changing. "Perhaps you should have a little work done—after all, you do know someone who can give you a stellar price!" Witty repartee?

Not really.

"Is my being 'plump', " Amelia asked, "a good reason for you to look elsewhere?" It was an odd question, but one that had been on her mind for quite some time.

"Oh, please, Amelia—all I said was you need to have a little work done. There's no reason to . . ."

"Bring up what I know to be true? After all, Thomas, it wouldn't be the first time . . ."

A well-placed shot.

Even so, dredging up unsavory behavior served no purpose other than to make Amelia feel better about herself—especially when she was guilty of the same thing. As much as she hated to admit her mistakes in life, the brief tête-à-tête her husband had with one of her closet friends was entirely Amelia's fault—and, Thomas never failed to remind her of her poor decisions. Especially the one when she decided to turn the tables by enticing Hector Cortina into her bed.

Clearly, fissures within the Sandoval marriage were deepening even though all parties worked out their issues nearly a year prior. Not only that, Thomas and Amelia did their best to squelch Friday night gossip by appearing to enjoy their marriage, especially when attending the Social Hour. But, a few knew otherwise . . .

Or, at least, suspected.

Was there the same tension in the Cortina household?

No one really knew.

By the time the Cortinas and Sandovals arrived, the Social Hour was in full swing. "You know I hate being late," Thomas hissed in his wife's ear as those they held dear turned to look.

Amelia said nothing, the sound of her husband's voice beginning to shred her ears. "Not now, Thomas," she whispered with a smile as they headed for the bar.

It was then both sensed a heaviness in the room, one uncustomary for Social Hour gatherings—and, it wasn't until Amelia noticed Hector's standing by himself like a teenage girl waiting for someone to ask her to dance, did she understand the magnitude of his legal problems. It made sense, too—earlier in the week, Hector's name was in the papers and social media again for protesting loudly against his dual arrests within the past month. The latest gossip, however, was more egregious than the first, Hector's circle deciding it was more prudent to step away from their friendship rather than encourage him to speak his truth. Their truth?

His friendship wasn't worth shit.

Of course, everyone speculated about reasons for Hector's arrests, but, salacious details had yet to be released to the press. A few suspected a gag order was in place, and it certainly would've been easy enough to determine—but, another truth?

No one really cared.

What Hector did was his business, and the majority of the Friday night Social Hour set honored his privacy. It was only a select few who took it upon themselves to learn the truth.

Yet they, too, remained silent . . .

As busy as South Beach was on a Friday evening, it was Decklin's good luck when he parked a mere hundred feet from one of the most palatial homes in the area. Since he only learned of Hector Cortina's marital duplicity a few days prior, he knew he had to continue his surveillance. Clearly, Hector wasn't a man to be trusted, so it also made sense if he had one secret, he probably had two.

Or, more.

Grateful that Analena didn't balk when he asked for the address of the get-together, Decklin smiled as he watched couples arrive for the Social Hour shortly after dark. A quick Internet search earlier that day revealed what he needed to know—the home belonged to a wealthy businessman who was a mainstay in South Beach. With a stellar reputation, there was little to be learned other than the usual—how he became successful despite his immigrant background.

A rags to riches thing.

But, while Aidan Lopez's story was interesting, there were many more who told the same story. What interested

Decklin most?

Who walked through Lopez's front door.

Elegant and classy, each guest was dressed in art deco style, complete with 1930's hairstyles and splendor. Obviously an upscale affair, Decklin immediately recognized Amelia Sandoval and her husband from photos lifted from the Internet. There was one guest, though, who caught his attention more than others—petite with spiky red hair, a middle-aged woman arrived alone, seeming out of place as Aidan Lopez greeted her.

Where's the costume, Decklin wondered as he watched her disappear through the home's front entrance.

Three hours later?

Out the door.

Keeping binos trained on guests as they left, again the redhead captured Decklin's attention as she climbed into a chauffeured black sedan. *Someone important,* he guessed as he pressed the ignition, then pulled away from the curb. *Everyone else arrived in their own cars . . .*

Unfortunately, that didn't mean squat when it came to figuring out what Hector Cortina was up to, prompting Decklin to return his thoughts to something more relevant. His first order of business?

Quality time with the Internet.

CHAPTER 6

*I*t's never fun when an important relationship goes belly up, so, when Decklin arrived home from his surveillance to find a note from Cecily on the foyer table, he knew it wasn't good.

A brief, handwritten note explained she needed time to think—to reassess their relationship—and, she was headed to her elderly aunt's home in upstate New York.

That should've been a stunner, but, if Decklin were honest with himself, her leaving wasn't much of a surprise. After moving south, both expecting to live out their lives in paradise, little in their relationship seemed to work, leaving Decklin to wonder if they made a mistake.

Apparently so.

But, after a good night's sleep, anxiety felt after reading Cecily's words was put in its place. *She'll call if she needs to talk*, he thought as he tackled the research necessary to identify Aidan Lopez's late night party guests shortly after arriving at his office.

By lunchtime?

With only four possible identifications, the red-haired woman remained a mystery. Of course, it was infinitely more difficult to identify someone on the Internet without a name, using only a photo he took with his phone. Realizing that, Decklin was kicking himself for not following the chauffeured vehicle as it left the party. He had an option, though . . .

Ask Analena Cortina who attended.

Preferring to make the call on his office phone, Decklin cracked a bottle of water, took a gulp, then punched in his client's cell number. After a brief greeting, he launched into the reason for his call. "I need a list of the people at the party you and Hector attended last night," he began, knowing she could shut him down before he could spit.

"Why do you need to know," she asked, failing to understand why those attending the previous night's soirée may have something to do with her husband's arrest.

"Analena," Decklin began, "your husband didn't get arrested for no reason—and, the fact he refuses to discuss it with you is cause for questions, don't you agree?" As Decklin heard his own words, he realized the time for placating the cosmetic surgeon's wife had come to an end. For having been on her payroll for more than a few weeks, he and Devon had little to show for their time.

Time to ignite the burner.

Decklin waited as Analena weighed his question. "Saying such a thing against my husband is difficult, Mr. Kilgarry . . ."

"Why? Are you afraid of something?"

Silence.

"I assure you, I won't break your confidence—so, if there's something I should know, now's the time."

Finally, Analena Cortina sighed, knowing her private detective was right. "There's much I question about my husband, Mr. Kilgarry—things that make little sense."

Decklin wasn't sure if she were talking about her husband's indiscretions or something else. *Perhaps she doesn't know about the woman who was with him at Rossi's,* he thought as he listened to another brief silence. *If that's the case, she needs to understand someone else is in her husband's life . . .* "What things, Analena? What doesn't make sense?"

For a second, Decklin wished he could carry on their conversation in person, but he recognized the anonymity of a phone call was probably more palatable for her. "It's always the same," Analena began to confide. "In the middle of the night he leaves, and I don't see him until it's time for dinner the next day . . ."

"Do you know where he goes?"

"No—and, my boys ask where he is." A pause. "I cry because I have nothing to tell them . . ."

In that moment, Decklin realized Analena Cortina was an ancillary victim—one unaware of things happening in her own life. "How often does he do that?"

"Twice a month, but never the same day or time . . ."

"What do you suspect?"

"Another woman . . ." Then, something unexpected. "He's done it before," she confided, her voice catching as she uttered the words.

"Do you know with whom?"

"Yes—Amelia Sandoval." Of course, it never occurred to Analena that Decklin and Devon already possessed what she thought would be bombshell information—and, in Decklin's mind, that was a good thing.

"How long ago?"

"Not quite two years—but, we got past it. At least, I thought we did—but, now? I'm not so sure . . ."

As Decklin listened, his gut churned knowing he must divulge to his client everything he knew so far about her husband—what he witnessed at Rossi's restaurant. "Well, Analena . . ." He paused, aware he must be direct and succinct—but, it was equally as important to deliver such news with compassion. "I followed your husband a few days ago because I, too, feel he's not being forthcoming about his arrest. But, what I learned has nothing to do with his arrest as far as I know . . ."

"Am I right, Mr. Kilgarry?"

A brief pause. "I suspect so—he met a young woman, and they went to Rossi's. Are you familiar?"

"With Rossi's? Oh, yes . . ."

Then, without consciously thinking about it, Decklin asked his next question. "So, I need to know—did your husband hire us? Or, did you? Hoping to find out the truth about him . . ."

Finally, Analena's resolve broke. "You are right, Mr. Kilgarry—I hired you, hoping you would find out what I need to know about my husband."

"You mean about his infidelity?"

"No—I was hoping to use that as an excuse."

"Meaning?"

"I think my husband is involved in something illegal—and, he has been for quite some time."

Decklin was quiet as he processed what his client was telling him. "Do you mean," he finally asked, "something other than the reason for which he was arrested?"

"Yes . . ."

Decklin paused, feeling their conversation was going in circles. "I'm afraid I don't understand, Analena—what is it you know?"

"Hector was arrested because he didn't go to court . . ."

"There was a bench warrant out for him? Why?"

"Because we are being sued—something I did not know until recently!"

As Analena spoke, Decklin realized she was nothing more than a wife who was kept in the dark about everything important. "Who's suing you," he finally asked.

So, after a five-minute explanation, it was clear Hector's arrest had nothing to do with anything nefarious—only a pissed off client who hated her new face. And, because of the warrant—which was unusual—Decklin suspected there was more to it. But, after Devon's research weeks earlier when he learned there were additional unsatisfied customers, Decklin knew his client was telling the truth.

Time to circle back.

"That at least answers one question for us—but, do you think Hector's leaving in the middle of the night has to do with his having an affair, or something else?"

Even though they were speaking by phone, Decklin could feel Analena's hesitation—then, a newly-surfaced confidence. "My marriage was in the toilet long ago," she suddenly confessed, the wronged-wife scenario suddenly taking a backseat to something more sinister. "And, though I'm not proud of it, I followed him one night . . ."

"When?"

"Just before I met Devon at the restaurant—in fact, I couldn't believe my luck when he told me about his business. With his being new in town, your partner seemed the perfect person to find out what's going on with Hector . . ."

Listening carefully, Decklin couldn't help noticing something different in her voice. Strong. Confident. "And, is that what you want Devon and me to do," he asked, uncertain of her answer. "Do you want us to find out what your husband does in the middle of the night?" A pause. "Is that the real reason you hired us?"

"Yes."

Connection severed.

Gisele Escalante stepped onto her back porch, the sun's warmth replaced by a cool fog cloaking the murky depths of the swamp. Her home for years, as much as she would've enjoyed something more in keeping with her true worth, maintaining an unassuming life was better suited to her mission.

What she was guided to do.

It is time, she thought as she scanned the fog's edge, drawing a small, lightweight table to her. Then, sitting on a generations-old stool, she opened one of its drawers, revealing two, nearly-spent candles, matches, and a cigar. In the other drawer, a black folder.

Scanning the darkness, she lit both candles, then opened the folder, gently extracting an eight-by-ten, full-color photograph, propping it against a claw-shaped piece of driftwood. Then, within the cloak of midnight and without anyone's noticing, she prepared to deliver her message.

With candles flickering in the cool, evening breeze, she lit the cigar, blowing its smoke at the photo until she could see the face no more.

Message delivered.

Though they weren't certain about what they were looking for, Decklin and Devon combed through the names of those attending Aidan Lopez's party, no one sparking interest. "Just rich people having a good time," Decklin finally concluded as he and Devon wrapped up work for the day. "The only person we know nothing about is the redhead I told you about . . ."

"You mean the one you let get away," Devon asked, grinning.

"Funny—but, yes. There's something about her that doesn't fit . . ."

"Well, you said she was alone, so that doesn't fit with the rest of them," Devon agreed. "Everyone else had a date or mate—so, why don't we try talking to someone who was at the party to find out who she is?"

"Good idea—I'm going to leave that to you. After conning a hostess to tell you about Amelia Sandoval, I think you're the man for the job!"

A returned grin. "Are you a betting man?"

"Not really," Decklin laughed, enjoying the camaraderie, knowing his partner would do whatever was needed to obtain information.

"Give me two days . . .

"Did you hear," Analena Cortina asked the following morning as soon as Decklin answered his cell.

Rubbing sleep from his eyes, he sat on the side of his bed, immediately concerned—she wasn't one for an early morning life, so, for her to call at such an hour?

It wasn't going to be good.

"They found Thomas . . ." Analena blurted, alarm in her voice. "Well, part of him . . ."

With that, Decklin was instantly awake. "Thomas Sandoval? And, what do you mean 'they found part of him?'"

"Yesterday—the ankle!"

Quickly clicking through events of the previous twenty-four hours, Decklin had no idea what she was talking about. "I didn't watch any news yesterday—what happened?"

A moment's silence as Analena collected herself. "Last night there was a story about finding a body part at the edge of the water—an ankle with a shoe still on it."

"And, you're saying the ankle belonged to Thomas Sandoval? How do you know that?"

"Well—that's what Amelia thinks. She told me Thomas has been gone for several days—and, when she checked with his office, they didn't know anything."

As he listened, Decklin realized Analena Cortina was easily swayed. "Did Amelia report him missing," he asked, hoping to play to her common sense.

It must've worked because instantly, Analena's voice morphed from anxious to questioning. "I don't know—I didn't ask."

"Well, if Amelia truly believes her husband is missing, the first order of business is to file an MPR—a Missing Person's Report."

"What happens after that?"

"We wait—there will be DNA tests, and it can take several weeks to get results."

So, with nothing more to say, Analena ended the call, leaving Decklin to wonder if he dreamed the whole thing.

It was interesting, though . . .

CHAPTER 7

Grinning, Devon placed a face-down photo in front of Decklin as he sat at his desk, jotting down notes regarding his early-morning conversation with Analena Cortina. "I told you I'd have an answer within two days . . ."

"You found her?"

"No—but, I know who she is!" Devon waited, enjoying the moment. "Well—turn it over!"

Gently, Decklin turned the photo over, grasping the picture as if it would turn to dust. "Holy shit! That's her!"

"I know! After I learned her name, everything from there was easy . . ."

"Okay—who is she?"

"Her name is Colbie Colleen—and, she's a professional profiler specializing in the paranormal."

"What?"

Both men were quiet, each sorting through personal thoughts. "What on God's earth," Decklin finally asked, "does a profiler specializing in something like that have to do with the upper crust of South Beach?"

A nod. "Exactly what I want to know . . ."

"What else do you know about her?" As Decklin focused on the photo, he couldn't ditch the feeling he and the redhead met previously—or, at the very least, she was within his awareness prior to his moving to Florida.

"Born in the Northwest, she obtained her degree in Psychology—after that, she had her own private investigation firm, working on important cases. Art theft and stuff like that—and, she's well-known within her circle." Devon paused, reading notes he took on his phone. "Several years ago, she attended Edinburgh University in Scotland, one of the few paranormal teaching institutions in the world. Well thought of, too . . ."

"Holy shit . . ."

"You know what I think," Devon asked, focusing his attention on his partner.

"Probably the same thing I'm thinking . . ." Decklin again looked at the photo, then at Devon. In unison, each spoke what they believed to be true . . .

"Santeria."

As weeks passed, Decklin couldn't stop thinking about why Colbie Colleen was in South Beach and, the more he considered the possibility, he was convinced their cases were overlapping. Even so, he had no idea how and where to get in touch with her. So, when he spied her standing on the corner waiting to cross the street on South Beach's main drag, meeting her was meant to be. Watching as she crossed, then pull on the door of a local bistro, he parked around the corner, then headed her way.

Once inside, he scanned the dining room—but, there were no patrons seated. *Damn! She couldn't have left already,* he thought as he stood next to the hostess stand. Then, a voice behind him. "Excuse me . . ."

Decklin turned, instantly recognizing the woman he saw when keeping eyes on those attending the Lopez gathering. "Yes?"

"Do you have the time?" A smile as she held up her wrist. "My watch died . . ."

Wanting to oblige while he dreamed up an excuse to have a conversation, Decklin returned the smile, glancing at his watch. "It's ten-forty five . . ."

"Oh—I guess I'll wait!"

Door opened.

"Well, we're both in the same boat, so why don't we wait together?"

A cheesy line.

Colbie smiled, then gestured to benches lining the restaurant's foyer. "Perfect!" Suddenly, she held up his pen. "This fell out of your pocket . . ."

Instantly, Decklin recalled sitting in the Ireland airport, waiting to catch a flight back to the States—the voice was the same. The smile.

The pen.

"I'm sure you don't recall," he commented as he took the pen, "but, I believe you and I have met before."

"Oh, I don't think so—I would've remembered!"

"The Ireland airport? You returned my pen when I dropped it?"

"Really?"

"Yep—your name is Colbie." Decklin paused, not taking his eyes from her. "I asked you your name as you walked away to catch your flight—and, you told me."

Ice broken.

So, agreeing to lunch together, it seemed Decklin was in an advantageous position, never thinking he'd have the opportunity to talk to Colbie Colleen about the reason she was in South Beach.

And, what an opportunity it was—by the time they were considering dessert, each knew the other's recent past, both enjoying the fact they were on the same side of the law.

They also knew to keep conversation light.

It wasn't until their lemon sorbets were a memory did they get down to things that mattered. "So," Decklin asked, "what brings you to South Beach?"

Knowing Decklin was a former D.C. detective played well, allowing the petite profiler a degree of trust. "I'm working . . ."

"Same—but, it feels as if I'm spinning my wheels. No matter what turn I take, it's the wrong direction . . ."

Colbie smiled, understanding how he felt. "I know what you mean—so, let's look at what you have so far." An offer she really didn't mean to make—what Decklin Kilgarry's case involved was none of her business, and the last thing she needed was something else on her plate.

"Seriously?" Decklin sat back in his chair, not quite believing his luck. Of course, their meeting was probably serendipitous, but, for some reason, it felt like more. "Okay—deal!" But, let's go somewhere that isn't quite so . . ."

"Air conditioned?"

"Exactly!"

Agreeing on a bench by the ocean's edge, within ten they sat, watching ships course the waters. "Okay," Decklin began, "my case . . ."

So, for the next hour they chatted, Colbie offering suggestions and, by the time they parted, they seemed like old friends. Cell numbers exchanged, both promised to be in touch soon . . .

Just not the following day.

It had been over three months since Cecily decided to visit her aunt in upstate New York, her absence silently declaring her relationship with Decklin was over. "I'm not happy when we're together," she stated bluntly the evening of Decklin's accidental lunch with Colbie Colleen.

Talk about timing.

But, he couldn't argue Cecily's reasons—he, too, recognized a chasm in their relationship, though he couldn't pinpoint exactly what went wrong. *Maybe,* he thought the following morning as he poured a glass of orange juice, *it just wasn't meant to be . . .* A fatalistic attitude? Yep.

But, it beat the hell out of feeling sorry for himself.

Fortunately, he put most of Cecily's belongings in storage and, though it was a hassle, Decklin agreed to ship everything to her aunt's.

Relationship done.

Of course, Decklin couldn't help wondering if the reason she left was because he couldn't get his shit together when it came to deciding how he wanted to live his life. In the beginning, Cecily was always in his corner—but, when he dissected their relationship, it wasn't hard to figure out things weren't all sunshine and lollipops—and, picking up stakes to move to Florida was nothing more than a Band-Aid.

"Movin' on . . ." he muttered as his cell chirped. Glancing at the screen as he put the orange juice back in the fridge, he instantly picked up.

"Colbie?"

No apology for calling so early. "I thought you might want to know, DNA results came back on the ankle . . ."

"What? How do you know?"

"Let's just say I have connections," she said, a smile in her voice. "It's Sandoval . . ." Then, the unexpected. "We have to meet . . ."

"I apologize for calling you so early—if you're anything like me during an investigation, you're up 'til all hours." Colbie glanced around her hotel lobby, making certain their conversation would remain private.

"That's not a problem—but, why do you want to meet?"

Colbie said nothing for a few moments, again weighing what she wanted him to know. "As of now, you're my colleague instead of a casual acquaintance . . ."

"Okay—tell me."

Again scanning the lobby, Colbie leveled her most serious look. "Tom Sandoval worked for us . . ."

Leaning back in his chair, Decklin simply looked at her, stunned. "He was embedded?"

A nod. "He'd been embedded in South Beach for years—you know, establishing himself. Marrying. Raising a family—all for the greater good, so to speak."

"You were working together?"

"Not exactly. I was brought in due to my—"

"Paranormal experience," Decklin interrupted.

Another nod. "How did you know?"

"My partner researched you when I saw you leave Aidan Lopez's cocktail party a few months ago. At least, I'm assuming that's what it was . . ."

"Close—it's what his circle calls the 'Social Hour.'"

"Explain . . ."

"Well, I don't know much—Tom was in their circle, so, when you saw me, it was the first time he invited me to attend." A pause. "Of course, my being there was nothing but a ruse, trying to glean information from people who hadn't yet stepped into my awareness . . ."

An interesting phrase, Decklin thought as he listened. "Did you learn anything new?"

Colbie shook her head, scanning the street outside the lobby windows. "No—and, that's why I'm coming to you. I'm thinking if we work the case together, we'll be much more successful. However, I understand if you'd rather go your own way . . ."

For the first time since he and Devon stepped into Analena Cortina's life, he felt as if he were in deeper than he anticipated. Every case was different, of course, but when the Feds were looking into the same things? When bringing in a psychic profiler?

All bets were off.

"So, what exactly is the Social Hour?" In Decklin's mind, he envisioned the socially elite bragging about themselves, caring more about their assets than what was important in life. "And, what's with the '30's costumes?"

"Oh, they're more than costumes! But, to answer your question, the Social Hour is a weekly get-together trying to recapture old Miami—you know, art deco. Hence, the way guests were dressed—and, you probably noticed I didn't participate."

"I did . . ."

"So . . . we've long suspected members of the Social Hour—for the last several years, anyway—are the nucleus of a group favoring Cuba over our own constitutional freedoms."

"You mean betrayal? Treason?"

"I suspect you know the answer to that . . ." Colbie smiled, then casually crossed her legs as if she were talking to someone about family recipes.

"Okay—but, why you? It doesn't seem your area of expertise—at least what I know of it."

"You're right, and that's why I wanted to meet—when recalling conversations with your client, did she mention anything you found unusual, outside of your usual investigative scope?"

Suddenly, remembering his conversation with Devon, the main reason for their meeting clicked. "Santeria."

Another smile. "Indeed . . ."

CHAPTER 8

*A*s one might imagine, Amelia Sandoval wasn't thrilled with the fact her husband's remaining body parts were most likely shark fodder— still, several weeks later, she insisted on a proper funeral, if not for her, for her children. "All I have is an ankle and his shoe," she lamented, not quite understanding what happened. "Do I need to buy a whole casket," she suddenly asked Analena when she stopped by to offer condolences.

Hector, conversely, was nowhere to be seen.

Among his peers, it was understood the good doctor only tolerated his primary competitor because he had to, and Sandoval's unfortunate passing was better for business.

Fewer competitors?

More money in Hector's pocket.

Luckily, Amelia had no idea who her husband's friends and colleagues were outside of a chosen few, making it easier for Decklin and Colbie to slip into the funeral two weeks later without drawing an inquisitive eye. Of course, Colbie had reason to be there since she was Thomas's invited guest to a Social Hour—Decklin, however? All he had was Analena, making his attendance unimportant—and, hopefully, barely noticed.

A mainstay to the South Beach community, Sandoval's devotion to his patients and country played well for him, the five hundred or so funeral guests singing his praises before and after the service. As they did, Colbie ventured off on her own while Decklin presented himself as one of Thomas's patients, all conversations nothing more than social platitudes. By the time it was said and done?

Nothing to show for their efforts.

But, as one might imagine, keeping track of five hundred funeral guests was nearly impossible, and what Decklin and Colbie missed?

Gisele Escalante slipping out a side door.

When thinking about it, only one thing is permanent within the guise of gossip—truth. After all, isn't that how gossip begins? With truth? Sadly, however, by the time more mouths were spewing the latest about Thomas Sandoval— and, in some circles, Hector Cortina—truth became skewed until it resembled nothing more than wishful thinking.

And, so it was with members of the Social Hour.

Of course, Thomas Sandoval's passing was met with condolences for those left to pick up the pieces—literally— but, it didn't take long to move on to something more salacious. More enticing. The obvious choice?

Hector.

Pivoting to Cortina's legal troubles seemed natural, especially since Hector and Thomas were in the same business of plumping and primping—so, within a few weeks, Thomas Sandoval was old news. Hector, however, managed to find himself a preferred topic of hushed conversations, and the first thing his Social Hour friends wanted to know?

Why Hector was really arrested not once, but twice.

Things probably would've died down with him, too, if it hadn't been for Analena. Appalled by Amelia's bad taste when questioning casket choices, Analena flat out told her it was none of her business when Amelia asked about Hector's surprise incarcerations. That, however, didn't seem to matter, and those who chose to keep gossip alive with Amelia at the helm morphed the whole thing into something Mrs. Cortina didn't recognize. Because of that, Hector's wife had only one thing on her mind . . .

Revenge.

"I don't care what you say," Decklin commented as Devon took a seat in his partner's office. "No woman wants to hear her husband is having an affair—and, that's why Analena initially hired us. Now, however, something else is afoot . . ."

"Agreed—but, does Hector's messing around with someone much younger really have anything to do with our case?"

Decklin eyed Devon, knowing he might be right. "Maybe—or, it could be merely salacious fluff. It's what we make of it . . ."

"Okay—so, what direction do you think we need to go? There's no question we're picking up steam, but I still have the feeling we don't know all of the players."

"I think you're right—and, that's why Colbie Colleen is embedded. For her to be involved, there has to be something more . . ."

Devon was quiet, not sure if he should ask about Decklin's most recent conversation with the paranormal profiler—but, since he and Decklin were partners, it made sense Devon should know. "What did you guys talk about when you saw her the other day?"

"A couple of things—the first is she wants to work with us. She thinks if we put our heads together, we can figure this thing out . . ."

"We—or, does that mean you? I can't imagine she'd want my input since I'm a newbie . . ."

Decklin shook his head. "Nope—she wants you in on everything." He paused as he thought about how he'd feel in the same situation. "I wouldn't have agreed if her suggestion didn't include you."

Devon grinned, the first time one hundred percent sure he made the right decision when accepting Decklin's offer to be partners. "That's what I want to hear!"

Toggling back to their case, Decklin knew he needed to discuss why Colbie Colleen was a part of the government's investigation. "They called her in because of the Santeria thing—do you have a problem with it?"

Devon sat back in his chair, clicking his pen—a nervous habit. "Well, I guess this is where the rubber meets the road—you know I don't like it, and the truth is the whole thing makes me nervous." A pause. "But—if I'm going to do my job, then I have to suck it up."

"Agreed—and, I admit, it makes me nervous, too."

"So—what does Colbie think is going on? She may have been brought in for her paranormal knowledge, but you and I know the government wouldn't be involved if there weren't something else."

"Treason."

A moment's silence. "Are you serious? Spy stuff?"

"That's what Colbie told me—and, Thomas Sandoval was embedded, too. That's how Colbie managed to attend the Social Hour—Sandoval invited her, hoping she would tune in or pick up on something."

More silence.

"What type of treason?"

"I asked Colbie the same thing—according to her, the Social Hour is the nucleus of a group favoring Cuba over our own constitutional freedoms."

"Geez . . ."

"I know—and, as you can imagine, this places our case on a whole different level."

"So, what's next?" Devon pushed forward, resting his forearms on the Decklin's desk. "Is Colbie going to handle the Santeria part?"

"I assume so—you and I can be of little help in that area. What we can do, however, is start turning the heat up on whomever we already think may be involved."

"And, they are . . ."

Decklin thought for a few seconds, mentally reviewing possible suspects. "I'm most interested in those who had the affairs . . ."

"Why?"

"Honestly? I don't really know—a gut feeling, I suppose."

When thinking about it, Decklin's gut feeling was more than Devon had. "Well, Hector is probably first on my list simply because he was arrested twice—and, he's having an affair with someone at least fifteen years his junior."

"Agreed—one thing we're sure of is Hector's propensity for making poor decisions."

"Maybe—certainly regarding the affair. But, his arrests were for something completely different—failing to show up for court doesn't exactly place him within our crosshairs."

Decklin agreed. "On the surface, I think you're right—however, the Fed's investigation has been going on for a long time. Thomas Sandoval was embedded in Miami for years."

"If that's the case, he must've known about the Santeria component, especially since Colbie was called in . . ."

"What's your point?" Decklin focused on his partner, interested in understanding his thoughts.

"Just this—Amelia Sandoval might know something. You and I know pillow talk is the private, personal stuff—and, I'll be willing to bet Thomas Sandoval left clues as to his real reason for living in Miami throughout their marriage."

Decklin stared out the window for a few seconds, instantly knowing their new trajectory was talking to the wives—as many as they could. "Excellent thinking, Devon—it makes sense." Suddenly, Decklin stood. "You're on Amelia Sandoval—stay with her."

"What about you?"

Decklin shoved notes into his manila folder, then locked them in his desk. "There's one person whom we haven't talked about yet—Aidan Lopez."

"The guy who hosted the Social Hour?"

A nod. "Yep—Thomas Sandoval was embedded in it, and it had to be for a specific reason. I'm figuring Lopez knows quite a bit . . ."

"How are you going to approach him?"

Decklin shook his head. "That, my friend, I don't quite know. So far, we haven't looked into his background—so, now's the time. I'll go from there." A pause. "In the meantime, you learn everything you can about Amelia Sandoval . . ."

"Roger that—and, if I find anything important, I'll message you."

In order to host a Social Hour, it made sense the person doing so was like-minded when it came to his guests—other than that? Decklin knew nothing about Aidan Lopez, so, it also made sense to contact Colbie about what she knew. "A quick meeting at the beach," he suggested when he contacted her by text midmorning.

Confirmed—#1 @ 11:00.

Prior to adjourning their last meeting, both agreed on certain spots they would meet, never going to the same one twice, if possible. That day? A little-known, privately-owned beach where few hung out, especially on a week day.

"Fancy meeting you here," Colbie commented with a grin as she sat beside him two minutes prior to their meeting time.

Grin returned. "How do you know about this place?"

"It's where Thomas and I used to meet—it's private, and posted as such in strategic spots."

"Ah—I didn't see the posts."

"That's because I told you a different route . . ."

"Well, then, that explains it!" Decklin laughed, the ease of talking to Colbie obviously enjoyable. "But, we only have a few minutes . . ."

A nod. "No more than fifteen minutes—and, I'll leave first." Suddenly, she rummaged through her messenger bag, extracting two sandwiches. "Here—if anyone's paying attention, we're simply enjoying each other's company over lunch . . ." Colbie scanned the beach in both directions, then focused on Decklin. "You hang out for another fifteen minutes or so after I leave. . ."

Obviously, there was little doubt about who was in charge of Decklin's and Devon's investigation—and, for about two seconds, the new Floridian wasn't sure he liked it. "Not trying to barge in on your case," Colbie offered, as if she were reading his thoughts. "But, since you're new to the area, I figured I can help when it comes to meeting locations— and, obviously, I have my own style when it comes to what I need a passerby to see."

"Works for me—so, let's get to the reason for our meeting. What does Aidan Lopez have to do with your case? Who is he?""

"Aidan Lopez is head honcho of a high seas shipping business based out of Miami . . ."

"Do you suspect he's involved?"

A nod. "That's something Thomas and I discussed many times, but, no matter how close he got to Lopez, the conversation stopped when it came to talking business."

"Even at the Social Hour when he was among his own?"

Colbie nodded, then took a bite of her sandwich. "Especially then. Lopez is—from what I could determine the one time I was there—the perfect host. Always laughing . . ."

"Interesting—it's my experience those who have a great business usually want to talk about it—you know, to bolster their own ego."

"I know."

"What's Lopez's background? Another rags to riches?"

Colbie laughed, then took another bite. "Eat your sandwich," she ordered with a smile. "We're supposed to be enjoying ourselves!" Then, a quick sip of water. "Exactly the opposite—the rags to riches, I mean. Aidan Lopez's father founded the business decades ago, eventually handing it over to Aidan when he took ill and could no longer run the company. Died seven years ago . . ."

"Did he have anything to do with illicit information being passed to Cuba?"

"Maybe—we don't really know."

"How old was he when he passed?"

"Ninety-three." Another bite. "Perhaps we should look into his background a little more," Colbie suggested. "I admit I haven't had the time—nor has my handler. But, I'll take care of it . . ."

"What's your gut," Decklin suddenly asked, hoping his questions weren't too intrusive. "About everything . . ."

Colbie finished nearly half of her sandwich, then squished the remaining crust into its paper wrapping as she glanced at her watch. "We're out of time," she advised as she stood, gathering her things. Then with a warm smile, she bade Decklin goodbye as if he were a dear friend. "Later . . ."

CHAPTER 9

isele knocked on the CEO's door, waiting for a directive to enter. "What do you want," he barked, a sure indication his day wasn't going well—clue number one.

"These came for you a few minutes ago," she advised, handing him three folders marked 'urgent and confidential,' each one sealed for insurance.

Aidan Lopez glanced at her with disdain, clue number two that something was amiss. "Did you open them," he asked without looking at her. Of course, he could've determined the answer to his question had he bothered to look at the envelopes. As it was, it was easier to pass his displeasure to the one person who kept his business operational.

"No—of course not."

Still without giving his operations manager the time of day, he dismissed her with nothing more than an irritated wave. "Go . . ." An insufferable boss?

No doubt.

Still, considering her salary, any personal degradation she had to suffer was worth it. Rising through the ranks, Gisele Escalante worked her way to the top over the years, eventually stepping into the number two position. It was her responsibility to keep operations running smoothly—a directive requiring knowledge of every facet of the operation.

And, it wasn't easy.

With shipping costs rising, it was up to her to make sure certain clients remained loyal and, those who did, were afforded preferential treatment coupled with under-the-table perks. In fact, Gisele was so successful at her job, competitors' bids to lure her away from Lopez were tempting, yet rarely considered.

She simply wasn't interested.

To most? Gisele Escalante wasn't a woman of means, and she made do with things she had, though she was always dressed to perfection. Not expensive—tasteful. At home, however?

A different woman.

Without bothering to inform Lopez she was heading home for the weekend, she stepped out of the shipping business's executive offices into cloaking humidity, grateful for its warmth on her skin. Air conditioning was something she was forced to endure and, according to her, it was the bane of her existence. But, as she looked forward to the evening's event, air conditioning and Aidan Lopez were the last things on her mind.

Grateful she had the building's number two parking space, Gisele lowered the windows as soon as she got behind the wheel, again enjoying the warm sea breeze and tropical humidity. Without waiting for the car to cool before driving, she tapped her cell screen three times. "Is everything ready for this evening," she asked, scanning the parking lot to make sure no one was close—a habit she couldn't shake.

"Yes."

"Perfect—we must be careful. I feel a shift . . ." Gisele glanced left and right in the parking lot as she pulled out of her space, then headed for the highway. "Things are changing, and we must be ready . . ."

"We will be."

"Excellent."

Connection severed.

She was right—there was a recent shift in energy, and anyone with the proclivity to perceive it would say the same. Though it was impossible to change her trajectory due to prior commitments, it was clear a certain negativity was beginning to stake its claim, and Thomas Sandoval's grisly passing was evidence of it. Was she in danger?

Probably.

But, none of that mattered—she had a job to do for only she could bring her mission to fruition, and that's exactly what she planned to do.

Still, she was concerned.

"Are you up for an adventure," Colbie asked, hoping Decklin would take the bait.

"Depends . . ." Then, a chuckle. "You didn't really expect me to say yes without knowing the particulars, did you?"

"Not really, but I'm always the optimist!"

As Decklin listened, he heard the smile in her voice—and, the truth was he was more than ready for an adventure. "What's up?"

"I just received word there's a ceremony I need to attend—surreptitiously, of course."

Well, that didn't sound good. "What kind of ceremony," Decklin asked, feeling as if he already knew the answer.

Colbie hesitated, uncertain if he were ready for what she had to say. "Santeria—as I said, I received information about a ritual ceremony this evening, and I'm thinking you may find it interesting."

As much as Decklin knew the ritualistic religion would come into their conversation again, he wasn't expecting it so soon. "As you know, I don't know the first thing about it . . ."

"You don't have to—I know enough for the both of us. I just thought you might want to learn more . . ."

"Okay—I'm in! When and where?"

"I'll pick you up at your office at eight o'clock—I'll text you when I arrive."

And, that was that.

Decklin watched his cell fade as an uneasy feeling settled in his stomach. *What did I just get myself into,* he wondered as he motioned to Devon to join him in his office. "I'm meeting Colbie at eight o'clock tonight—she's taking me to a Santeria ritual ceremony," he advised his partner before he sat down.

"Are you—"

"Nuts? Probably. But, I figure the more I learn about the underpinning of this case, the better off we'll be . . ."

"I don't have to go, do I?"

"No—and, I don't think there's a reason for you to go. I know it makes you uncomfortable—and, the only reason I'm going is because Colbie asked me to. I doubt she'd do that if she thought it would make me feel uncomfortable about the whole thing."

Devon said nothing for a few moments as relief coursed through every vein. "Good—I'm okay with letting you handle it!"

So, for the next few minutes they discussed the case, plus a new one that was possibly on deck. "Go ahead and take off," Decklin finally suggested. "I'm going to work here until Colbie picks me up . . ."

"I'm available if you need me . . ."

A portend?

Could be.

But, Decklin didn't want to think about it.

Stepping out of his office building doors just as Colbie's driver pulled up to the curb, the sleek, black SUV telegraphed she was someone important—perhaps, more important than he originally thought. "So glad you're joining me," she said with a smile as the driver held open the backseat's passenger door, then took his place behind the wheel. "I'm glad I didn't scare you off!"

"Nope—I'm always up for learning something new!"

"Excellent!" A pause as Decklin buckled up. "I'd like you to meet Anderson—my driver for the time I'm in Florida." With a salute and a nod, Anderson smiled as he focused on Decklin in the rearview mirror. "He's usually an office geek, but, for this operation, the brass decided it's a good idea to have someone with me as we go forward." Probably an easy choice, too—Colbie's colleague-turned-driver looked as if he could bench press three hundred pounds.

Though her comment was meant to quell any uncertainty, it wasn't exactly what Decklin wanted or needed to hear. "I'm glad they're putting your safety first," he finally replied, not enjoying a rising unease.

"They always do—but, enough of that." Colbie paused, looking out the window as if mentally cataloguing every passing landmark. "Let's go over what we're getting ourselves into . . ." Focusing on him, she easily read what he was feeling. "I promise if you're uncomfortable, we'll leave—but, I suppose I should mention we'll be out of sight."

"What?"

A nod. "Yes—we'll be watching from the periphery, learning what we need to know." What she didn't tell him?

They'd be hidden by jungle foliage, only accessed by a little-known trail from the location's backside.

"Maybe I should've changed clothes," Decklin joked, hoping she wouldn't detect his nerves.

Soon after arriving at their destination, Anderson led them to an overgrown trail, making certain all was as it should be. "This is good," he finally advised. "Send the code if there's trouble . . ."

The code? Shit . . . Again wondering what he got himself into, Decklin said nothing as Colbie agreed. Watching as Anderson forged his way back to their vehicle, Decklin couldn't help feeling a bit envious that Anderson got to spend time in the car.

"We have five minutes before the ritual begins," Colbie commented as they approached their location—but, as you can see, the fire is already ignited."

And, so it was.

Decklin and Colbie watched from their cover among overgrown, wet jungle leaves as those taking part in the ritual painted their chests with white paint, the flames casting eerie shadows upon their already decorated faces. "Are those symbols on their chests," he asked, watching, as if mesmerized by the flames.

"Yes . . ." Colbie glanced at him, then focused again on the preparations for the ritual. "In Santeria, 'orishas' are gods or beings with whom believers interact on a regular basis—and, the number of orishas varies among believers."

"Okay . . ."

"And," she continued, "Santeria originates from an original African belief system—there are hundreds of orishas. The 'New World Santeria' believers, however, generally work with only a few of them, and what we're witnessing now is part of the newer Santeria."

"It looks a lot like voodoo to me . . ."

"I know—but, it isn't. Suffice it to say people from West Africa emigrated to Cuba and, from that fountain, Santeria was born. Still, it's African magic, some of it harmful . . ." Suddenly, Colbie placed her finger to her lips. "It's starting."

From their position among the trees, Decklin and Colbie watched as a processional appeared from the shadows, comprised of several men and a few women. "Who's she," Decklin whispered.

"The High Priestess. " Again, a finger to her lips. "More later . . ."

Silent, both watched, the striking woman in white greeting attendees as ignited torches illuminated painted faces of those surrounding her. Speaking to her followers, she explained the reason for their gathering, then led worshippers in chanting to the beat of two drums for more than an hour. "Do you feel a shift in the energy," Colbie whispered to Decklin.

"No."

"Well, that's what she's been doing for the last hour—redirecting energy."

Decklin said nothing, watching worshippers finally step back into the shadows as the High Priestess disappeared into the jungle along a secluded trail.

"It's done," Colbie finally commented as she texted Anderson. "Let's go . . ." Silent and using the small flashlight

Anderson slipped to her without Decklin's noticing, they made their way down the path and, as they arrived at their pick-up location, the SUV came into view. "Well, that was interesting," Colbie commented as Anderson rolled to a stop, no longer feeling the need to whisper. "What do you think, Decklin?"

"Well, as interesting as all of it was, I'm not sure why we were there—other than a learning experience for me."

"That was part of it . . ." A leading statement?

Of course.

"What's the other part?"

"I wanted you to see my colleague in action." Colbie couldn't help smiling at Decklin's expression of complete confusion.

"I don't understand . . ."

"The High Priestess—Gisele Escalante. She receives and moves information for us . . ."

Stunned, Decklin instantly recognized the name. "Analena Cortina mentioned her in one of our initial meetings . . ."

"Really? In what context?"

Quickly, Decklin cycled the conversation with Analena through his brain. "She thinks Gisele is responsible for Hector's being arrested—and, she also thinks Escalante threw a curse on him." A pause. "In fact, that's how I learned about Santeria's being a possible link in our investigation."

Colbie turned sideways to face him. "Well, you're right about that—Santeria is instrumental, but not in the way you might think."

"Tell me . . ."

"We've long-suspected the Mexican cartel has infiltrated the Cuban community in Florida—specializing in what they do best, of course."

"Trafficking."

"Exactly—and, not just drugs. Human trafficking is gaining in popularity with them, and they pride themselves on being well-rounded when it comes to making money."

"And, lots of it—so, how does Gisele play into it?"

"In order to do her job effectively, she embedded in the shipping business—in particular, Allied International Shipping."

"Why?"

"Because of who owns it . . ."

Decklin waited for a few seconds, thinking Colbie would continue. When she didn't, he had to wonder why. "And, that person is?"

"None other than Aidan Lopez."

"Ah—the Social Hour guy."

"One and the same. Do you recall our talking about it when we had lunch a few days ago? When you wanted to know about Aidan Lopez?"

A nod.

"I wasn't comfortable telling you everything until I cleared it with brass—but, there's definitely a shift in the energy"

"You mean things are going to start moving with your case?"

"Yes—intel has it there's discussion among the ranks about the cartel's taking advantage of the current political climate in Washington D.C."

"That wouldn't surprise me—I worked that arena for decades, and it's nothing more than a cesspool of corruption."

"My brass agrees—unfortunately, we also can't trust some of our own. We know there's treasonous information being passed—but, unfortunately, it takes a long time to put a case together. Surveillance alone can take months—or, years."

So, with that information to go on, they parted ways, Anderson dropping off Decklin in front of his office building, Colbie promising to be in touch.

Not exactly stuff for a good night's sleep.

CHAPTER 10

*F*or a woman scorned, exacting revenge is tricky business—if not executed with precision and intent, the whole damned thing could wind up a hot mess.

Exactly what Analena Cortina didn't need.

Of course, what turned her thoughts to getting even was her husband's spending quality time with Florida's finest, refusing to confide possible reasons for his unanticipated incarceration. Instead, he chose to alienate her, all the while spending time with a woman whom Analena didn't know.

Both reasons for revenge.

As much as she wanted to bring a confidant into her plans, Analena soon realized doing such a thing wasn't particularly bright. Her reasoning? Most of her friends couldn't help flapping their jaws about most things, so entrusting one of them to help her with dirty work wasn't the best choice. In fact, the only one who might be acceptable was Amelia Sandoval—and, she was a crapshoot at best. Over passing weeks, their friendship was on the skids, neither enjoying the other's company, and there was something unsettling lodging in Analena's mind.

So, armed with a recording app on her cell, her plans commenced with only one acceptable resolution.

Take Hector Cortina for everything he was worth.

Yes, it was a lofty goal, but, to Analena's thinking, it was well-worth what would undoubtedly be a psychologically damaging ascent to freedom. The more she considered an unencumbered life for her and her children, the more she knew she was doing the right thing. She certainly must've been because she convinced herself of it every day since she learned Hector was nothing but a no-good cheat. A mighty motivation, indeed.

The only thing she needed?

An opportune time.

Fortunately, it wasn't difficult to learn Hector's patient schedule, his last one scheduled no later than four o'clock—info learned from his chatty receptionist. That meant Hector would leave shortly after four-thirty, which Analena figured was a perfect time for surveillance on a balmy Friday afternoon. *The boys are at soccer,* she thought as she cycled through her plan, *and won't be home until after six . . .*

Just enough time.

So, precisely at four-fifteen, Analena Cortina parked across the street from her husband's office building primed to prove herself right about everything.

And, she didn't have to wait.

A few minutes after four-thirty, Hector exited the building with a shit-eatin' grin on his face as he headed toward the parking garage, his smile something Analena rarely had the pleasure of enjoying. *What's that all about,* she wondered as she watched through tiny binos that fit perfectly in her designer clutch.

Minutes later, his McLaren 720S pulled into the afternoon sun, turning left onto South Beach's main drag, the ocean's scent and breeze making him feel like a million bucks. What else made him feel like a million bucks?

An afternoon tryst with a young woman of choice.

Ten minutes later, the woman Decklin Kilgarry described to Analena a few weeks prior met him at the street corner, a delightful smile pasted on her face as he waited for her to climb in and fasten her seatbelt. As she watched, Analena realized the young woman was someone she didn't know, sparking her to wonder how he met her in the first place. Their destination? A swanky hotel on the south end of the island.

Watching as Hector and his lady friend disappeared through the hotel's doors, there were few rational possibilities remaining—and, it was that moment of clarity solidifying what a wife must do when faced with such realities. It was also when Analena Cortina's resolve confirmed what she must do . . .

No matter the consequences.

One thing Decklin Kilgarry learned from the demise of two important relationships was to always be present—a buzz word he heard more than once over the past several months when Cecily was figuring out where life would take her. *What the hell does that even mean,* he questioned as he sat on his condo's small balcony, beer in hand. *But, it sure as hell must mean something since I managed to squander the one good thing in my life . . .*

Was he feeling sorry for himself?

A little.

But, truth can scorch a soul, and he was well-aware he could've handled things differently with Cecily—he also knew it was too late to resurrect what needed to stay buried. So, when Colbie texted a message to meet her for dinner at an out-of-the-way barbecue joint on the outskirts of the city, how could he refuse? "Okay—I'm here! I gathered from your voice there's something important we need to discuss outside of technological devices . . ."

"Correct," Colbie admitted as the hostess guided them to an outdoor table. "Let's get settled, then we'll talk . . ."

A few minutes later, refreshing drinks in front of them, Colbie sat back in her rather uncomfortable chair, focusing on the man across from her. "You're troubled," she began, her tone leaving little room for countering her observation.

"It's that obvious?"

"Yes . . ."

Decklin said nothing, hesitating to confide his thoughts from earlier that afternoon. After all, Cecily left no room for reconciliation—still, her absence hurt his heart no matter how much he tried to tell himself differently. "It's nothing," he commented, knowing no good could come of such a conversation.

"I understand—so, on to other things!" Raising her glass in a half salute, she scanned the restaurant's patio. "Who's the woman Hector Cortina's seeing . . ."

Decklin frowned, slightly surprised she knew. "I don't know—I only learned of it recently. While I suspect he's involved romantically, I don't have confirmation or a name." A moment's silence. "Why? Is she involved in your case?"

Colbie shrugged slightly, then took a sip of her cocktail. "Yes, and no—we only received word a couple of days ago that Cortina is seeing someone. I figured you might know something . . ."

"Well, I can tell you when I surveilled Hector not too long ago, he met a young woman, then headed for Rossi's Italian restaurant."

"I don't know it."

A smile. "I can see why—it's an out of the way hole-in-the-wall that's seen better days. Chances of being recognized there are probably slim . . ."

Placing her cocktail glass on the table, Colbie said nothing until she was certain of what needed to happen next. "We have reason to believe she's involved with the Mexican cartel—her name is Gloria Fuentes."

"If you already knew, why ask?" As the words came out of Decklin's mouth, he instantly regretted their tone. "I'm sorry, I didn't mean . . ."

"No apology necessary—and, to answer your question, I wanted to know if you and I were talking about the same person. It appears Hector may be involved with more than one . . ."

Well, that was news.

"Based on . . ."

Colbie shook her head. "I'm sorry, but that's info I can't divulge. I'm sure you understand . . ." Honestly, though?

Decklin didn't understand.

Maybe it was because he'd been feeling sorry for himself for the entire day. Even so, something didn't sit right when Colbie refused to take him into her confidence, though he understood her perspective from his experience as a homicide detective. Still, if they were going to work together, shouldn't he know everything?

Apparently not.

"So, what do you know about Gloria Fuentes," he asked, trying to keep his tone more in line with their goal.

A smile. "The fact you already got eyes on her is to your credit—as far as I know, they've only been seen together in public a couple of times. Excellent work . . ."

"Much appreciated—but, seeing them together wasn't by design. I was surveilling him, and I got lucky . . ."

"Maybe—but, as I'm getting to know you better, I'm clear on your needing time to get your thoughts straight about a case before mentioning anything to anyone." A pause. "Am I right?"

As Decklin sat across from her, he was becoming acutely aware of her intuitive capabilities—and, it was making him slightly uncomfortable. During his time on the force, he worked with psychics on a few occasions, but none were anything like the woman with whom he was dining. Then, a smile. "You're on the money—I like facts before conversation!"

"That's good—and, it's one of the things convincing me I can trust you as we move forward with the case. Already, you managed to provide information, and you're a good addition to the cause—if I had my way, I'd tell you everything we know."

"I appreciate your confidence . . ."

Colbie was quiet, sensing Decklin's discomfort with the conversation—time to pivot. "So—Gloria Fuentes. Twenty-eight years old and the daughter of a noted Mexican cartel boss, we know she's assuming her father's position in the near future."

"Interesting—do you think she's playing Hector?"

Colbie shook her head. "No—we think she's instrumental in passing information to the Cuban government."

"Through Hector?"

A nod. "Chatter is ramping up, and the content of intel is becoming more troublesome."

"In what way?" Decklin leaned forward just in case a passing server took notice of their conversation.

"I can't go into particulars, but it's important we learn exactly what part she's playing with Hector . . ."

Decklin thought for a minute, cycling through their suspect list. "I swear every week our players change—so, who do you have on your radar?" Though Decklin thought he knew, he needed to make sure they were on the same page.

Question ignored.

Colbie waited until their server placed their meals in front of them, offering a smile and a compliment before the young woman left her guests to their business. "She's very good—not intrusive," Colbie noted, surveying her plate.

After agreeing to table their discussion until dessert, it was the first time each had the opportunity to get to know the other. "So," Decklin began, "I don't know anything about you other than what's on the Internet—what do I need to know that isn't publicly stated?"

Without taking a moment to think, Colbie instantly answered. "I believe we're the keepers of our own destinies and success—it's ours to win or lose."

Not exactly what Decklin expected—all he really wanted to know was a bit about her past. Her answer, however, revealed thinking of a person who chose to delve into the depths of her identity—and, it was then he understood. "I agree—we become fallible because of our frailties, and steeled when we speak and act out of need for success."

"Yes—except, that can be a bit of a trap, don't you think?" Without waiting for an answer, Colbie continued. "I mean, if you look at Hector Cortina, he's the product of his own greed. His own desire for success—one that morphed into something sinister."

"Agreed—so what's Hector's backstory?"

A nod. "Good question—Hector Cortina wound up on our radar through an email he sent ten years ago to Juan Fuentes."

"Let me guess—Gloria's father?"

Another nod. "Yep—one and the same."

"I'm assuming you know the content of said email . . ."

"Yes—the first one we intercepted was due to a conscientious whistleblower, one who's in our protection program—in fact, if it weren't for that person, we'd probably still be in the dark."

As Decklin listened, he began to connect the dots. "Just from what you commented about Gloria's father, I'm guessing he may be around the same age as Aidan Lopez."

Colbie smiled, then took a final bite of her dinner. "He was older. Interestingly, we had the same thought—and, our suspicions were verified, but not immediately. It took surveillance and an eventual clandestine meeting between Lopez and Juan Fuentes to stir the embers of what had been simmering for a long time. After that, it was only a matter of time before we had operatives in place—and, they've been in place for quite a while."

"How close are you to making an arrest?"

Colbie shook her head as she sat back in her chair, placing her napkin on the table. "Well, we're getting closer, but we still have a lot of work to do—due to cutbacks in Washington, we don't have the manpower to do our best. So, it was a godsend when you and Devon showed up . . ."

Decklin smiled, enjoying the compliment. "So, what's the story . . ."

Suddenly, Colbie got up, signaling their time was up. "We've been here for an hour—time to go."

Suppertime over.

CHAPTER 11

*J*uan Fuentes eyed his daughter, dissatisfaction settling as he knew he must address what could only be described as irresponsible actions. "You're playing with fire, Mija . . ."

Gloria glared at him, her father's intimation clear—yet, she knew she mustn't speak her mind. "I don't know what you're talking about—I haven't done anything other than what you ask of me."

A nod. "That's true—but, you're not taking responsibility for what will soon be yours! How can I leave you, knowing my empire is at risk due to your foolishness?"

"What am I to do? I have no authority—at least not as long as you're directing operations!"

Silent, her father didn't take his eyes from her, wondering if he made a mistake when tagging his daughter for his next-in-line rather than his sister's boy—his nephew. Recognizing she had a point, he realized she must be brought into the fold differently. "You have a relationship with him?"

Gloria blushed, delivering her answer without words.

"Exactly what I thought!" Juan paused, fully aware how such an attraction could prove fatal. "He can give you nothing, Mija! It is you who must take everything from him!"

"You misunderstand—I want nothing from him but information. How better to persuade a man than through his bed?"

A statement Juan recognized as truth.

"He brags about his business," Gloria continued, and it won't be long until his words raise suspicion among the wrong people. If that happens?"

It was then Juan Fuentes realized his mistake. "I apologize, Mija, for underestimating you, but surely you understand my concern . . ."

It was a valid one, too. Ever since Gloria was a child, she exhibited a certain bent for caring about others, a personal trait that could get her in trouble when in the right circumstances. "I do," she confirmed, "but, I have no interest in Hector Cortina—once I find out what we need to know, his service to us will be over."

"Are you certain he's betraying our trust?"

A brief silence. "Yes—but, I don't know anything else. Since he doesn't know me as your daughter, however, I'm certain I can convince him to take me into his confidence."

"He's that stupid?"

Gloria laughed, enjoying the role she was playing with the man who could bring her father's organization down. "Oh, yes!"

"Then, your job is simpler . . ."

Gloria rose from the family table, crossed to a small bar, then poured her father a drink. "Make no mistake, Papá— I'm prepared to do what's needed to save our business. But, I feel walls closing in and, now, we need to plan."

A heavy sigh as Juan accepted the glass. "My time is short, and we must protect ourselves. My only option is to trust you . . ."

"You can trust me, Papá . . ." As Gloria turned from him, a smile tugged at her lips. Surely, she played her part well, her father believing every word—and, telling him only what he needed to know was fitting into her plans beautifully. *I will rise,* she thought, knowing he was nodding off after only one sip of his drink.

And, I will do great things . . .

"How was your day," Analena asked as Hector walked through the door after dark, expecting his dinner. "You're home late . . ."

"I had a meeting after seeing patients . . ."

A lie.

It's probably difficult to carry on a conversation with someone who lies—at least, that's what Analena learned after listening to her husband utter one sentence. "Where was the meeting," she asked, refusing to sit with him at the dining room table.

"The Tropics . . ."

Another lie.

But, one more didn't matter.

Smiling, Analena placed his dinner plate in front of him. "It's been a long day, and I'm tired . . ." So, with nothing else left to say, she left the dining room, knowing her life was about to change. *All in good time, Hector . . .*

All in good time.

As far as Decklin was concerned, there was nothing better than a gloomy day in the office, offering a coziness he particularly enjoyed. "So, what did you learn about Amelia Sandoval," he asked Devon after giving his young partner time to grab a cup of coffee.

"It's interesting, that's for sure!" Devon placed his mug on the conference room table, then joined Decklin. "First, though, tell me about you—why did Colbie want to meet with you?"

For the next fifteen, Decklin recounted the Santeria ritual, leaving nothing to his partner's imagination. "And," he continued, "the High Priestess of the ritual was none other than Gisele Escalante . . ."

"Isn't that who Analena said cursed Hector?"

"One and the same . . ."

Devon said nothing, knowing what he had to tell Decklin would blow him out of the water. "Well, you're never going to believe where Amelia went that same night . . ."

"Tell me . . ."

"The same Santeria ritual."

Stunned, Decklin instantly recognized a connecting thread. "Was she simply an observer," he asked, though he knew that most likely wasn't the case. There were a few people on the fringe of the ritual, but none were Amelia Sandoval.

"Nope—in fact, I thought I lost her when she pulled into a sandy parking area, then disappeared. But, I decided to hang out to see if I could pick her up again when she returned to her car—and, I did, but, she wasn't the Amelia I was tailing."

"Meaning?"

"She was covered in face paint—symbols, I think—but, I couldn't really tell since I was across the road. Her clothes were different, too . . ."

"Are you telling me she took part in the Santeria ritual?"

Devon took a sip of coffee, then placed his mug on the table. "It seems so . . ."

"If that's the case, there's a connection we didn't know about—and, an important one."

"I'm guessing you're talking about her husband?"

"Exactly—it makes me wonder if Thomas Sandoval knew of his wife's religious preference."

"How could he not? I learned through my research it's a belief system—how could her husband not know?"

As both men settled into the rhythm of rain splatting on their office windows, each instinctively knew Thomas Sandoval was aware of his wife's Santeria ritual practices. The real question?

Did he care?

Scrutinizing her reflection in the bathroom mirror, Carmen Santosa couldn't help feeling the same rage as when Hector Cortina removed the bandages after her last surgery. Gone was her youthful appearance, replaced by the unmistakable duck lips, high cheekbones, and skin resembling warm plastic stretched to capacity. Not a good look . . .

And, she knew it.

The whole thing was really too bad—after all, Carmen liked Hector, enjoying his company each time she decided she needed a lift. You know—a boost making her feel better about her own DNA. The daughter of a Cuban diplomat, she felt she had a certain image to maintain. So, at the tender age of thirty-nine, it was time to correct what nature ignored, and it didn't take her long to walk through Dr. Cortina's door.

A pricey venture.

At first, they were cordial with each other, but, as cosmetic procedures mounted, both discovered a mutual admiration for the Cuban government. One thing led to another and, before both knew it, they formed an allegiance, neither confirming their political preferences. Yet, both would do what was required for their home country. Unfortunately, when Hector couldn't adequately repair what he termed a mere 'slip of the knife,' their friendship tanked, and Hector wound up coughing up a cool million.

Analena never the wiser, of course.

Peering intently into her gilded mirror, all Carmen Santosa saw was imperfections. Of course, it didn't take a genius to figure out self-perceived deficiencies were nothing more than surfacing signals of a tortured soul—an observation Carmen refused to admit. She much preferred simmering anger aimed at the one person whom she thought she could trust.

Suddenly, she pulled back, a tight smile refusing to offer a glimpse of her teeth. In a moment of clarity she instantly knew what she must do if she were to be true to her allegiances. *Enjoy what you have, my friend . . .*

Enjoy.

Much like his father, Aidan Lopez preferred to sequester himself away from the masses, offering no time to those who could've benefited from his presence. So, when Juan Fuentes showed up unannounced on a Thursday afternoon demanding to see the top dog, there was little doubt something was up.

Quietly, Gisele placed her out-to-lunch sign on the door, then locked it from the inside—if Lopez or Fuentes commented, all she had to say was the placard was placed for their own best interest. *Who can argue against privacy,* she thought as she sat at her desk, then removed tiny, wireless earbuds from a drawer. Moments later, she listened to her boss's voice in her ear, his tone one of displeasure. "You look unwell, my friend . . ."

Juan nodded, knowing it was time to discuss the salient points of their business together. "I have limited time, I'm afraid . . ."

Lopez said nothing, silently weighing the probable consequences associated with Juan's proclamation. Then, the perfect response, though it was a bit generic. "I'm sorry to hear . . ."

"Such is life, my friend—but, I didn't come here to speak of my health." Fuentes paused, choosing his words carefully. "As you know, my passing will affect many within our organizations, and it is my duty to keep our mutual clients happy."

Aidan shifted in his chair, uncertain if he wanted to hear what Lopez had to say. Of course, when a patrón—a godfather of sorts—is in the situation of making decisions regarding all business, each aspect affecting the bottom line must be considered. "I assume you've made arrangements, yes?"

"Of course—at my passing, my daughter will be in charge of all operations. Gloria . . ."

Just what Aidan Lopez didn't want to hear.

Gloria Fuentes had a widespread reputation among their mutual operatives, none of it good. "You're certain she's the best choice?"

A smile. "You doubt?"

"No—but, she's young, and I do wonder how those on my end of our arrangement will feel about working with her." Aidan focused on Juan, his eyes belying unspoken concern. "I'm sure you understand . . ."

"My daughter is well-qualified—and, I've taught her well. As far as I'm concerned, the arrangement we have in place must stand . . ."

"Indeed—for it makes us rich, mi amigo!" Laughing, Lopez opened his desk drawer, extracting two Cuban cigars, handing one to Juan. "To celebrate the continuation of our agreement," he declared as he snipped the end of his own, then waited for his guest to do the same.

"There is one more thing," the cartel leader advised, taking a moment to puff the cigar to life. "Something causing concern . . ."

"Which is?"

"It has come to my attention, there's movement among our enemies, and we must be careful of every word. Every deed. . ."

That didn't sound good.

Again, Aidan shifted, uncomfortable with the direction their conversation was heading. "What do you know . . ."

A prolonged pause. "Hector Cortina is choosing a path uncharitable to both of our organizations—and, if such information is true, we must take action to protect our respective and individual interests." As Juan spoke, veiled, dark intention deadened his eyes, his voice acquiring an unpleasant edge.

"What is your suggestion?" Although it sounded a bit lame, Lopez's question was on the money, and a half-wit would know just by looking at Juan, he had a plan in place.

As the men spoke, Gisele recorded their conversation, recognizing it as essential intel—information she must pass to her contact. Quickly, she sent a text, not expecting a reply, knowing what her evening would hold . . .

A momentary, clandestine meeting.

CHAPTER 12

Watching his cell screen fade, Decklin figured he wouldn't receive an answer quickly. Within a few minutes, however, a notification chirped, providing a reply to his question.

Rossi's. Six-thirty . . .

Smiling, he checked his watch, realizing he had time for a quick shower. Why Colbie wanted to meet at the restaurant where he spied on Hector Cortina and Gloria Fuentes, he didn't know. He was, however, up for an evening outside of his condo.

Within the hour, he pulled on Rossi's door, noting Colbie was waiting at a table smack dab in the middle of the restaurant. "So you can see everything going on," Decklin asked, knowing she would understand.

"Nope—I just don't want to appear as if we have something to hide." As she spoke, Colbie scanned the restaurant, pleased there were about twenty customers throughout.

Decklin noticed. "The more people, the better, I always say!" Pulling out a chair, he also noticed the petite redhead was dressed as if she just stepped off the beach.

"Agreed." She waited until he sat, then handed him the wine list. "Anything suit your fancy," she asked, watching as he glanced at the list.

"Merlot—perfect for Italian, don't you think?"

"My favorite!"

So, with that, they were off, each mentally cataloguing everyone who walked through the door—and, by seven o'clock the place was packed. With dinner entrées on the way, Decklin finally got to the reason he wanted to meet with her. "As I continue to roll everything we know around in my brain, there's one thing that's bugging me . . ."

"And, that is?"

"Someone has to be passing intel from inside of our government—so, do you know who?"

"No. We suspect, but we don't have proof—and, you know as well as I, without the goods we don't have anything."

"Can you tell me who?"

For the first time in their working relationship, Colbie appeared conflicted. Putting herself in Decklin's place, she wouldn't like it one bit if pertinent information were kept from her. "I'm not at liberty to say . . ."

Silence.

"However, I think if we're to work together, it's important we're honest. Over the past few weeks, you demonstrated your professionalism, and I have no doubt I can trust you."

"I appreciate it."

Colbie took a beat as she considered how much to reveal and, after a few moments, she knew she must bring Decklin up to speed on everything. "We suspect a U.S. Embassy translator for our government . . ."

"Name?"

"Carmen Santosa."

Decklin was quiet for a few moments, searching his memory banks. "I'm sure the name hasn't come up in our investigations . . ."

"I'm not surprised—we've had her in our sights for a while, but there's nothing compelling enough to motivate us to move at this time."

"Do you happen to have a photo of her," Decklin asked, knowing he was more effective when having a visual representation.

Colbie nodded, tapping her cell to life. "I shouldn't have this on here," she confessed as she handed her cell to him. "Take a good look because it'll be gone—I'll transfer it to a thumb drive, then delete it."

As Decklin studied the photo, something seemed odd about the blonde, brown-eyed woman, but he couldn't quite figure it out. "Of course," he finally commented, "her hair is bleached, but there's something that's not right . . ."

"What do you mean?"

"Honestly, I'm not sure. She looks . . . fake."

As soon as Decklin spoke, Colbie knew instantly what he was interpreting. "She's Hector Cortina's patient . . ."

A grin. "That explains it! It makes me wonder, though, what she looked like before the work." Decklin took a moment to scrutinize the photo, then passed the cell back to Colbie. "Doesn't look good to me . . ."

"In the eye of the beholder, I suppose . . ."

It wasn't until they were about to leave Rossi's when a light flicked on in Decklin's brain. "You probably have a better understanding of the cosmetic surgery business than I . . . "

"Excuse me?"

Decklin blushed, suddenly realizing how his words sounded. "Oh, geez! I didn't mean it that way!"

Colbie smiled, taking a last sip of her merlot. "I know—I was just giving you the business."

"I meant—"

"I know what you meant—it's okay!"

"Well, Ms. Colleen, you can expect payback!" Decklin placed his napkin on the table as if laying a gauntlet.

As Colbie followed suit, he rose, then pulled back her chair as she stood. It had been a long time since he had the opportunity to display his childhood upbringing, and he enjoyed it.

Something Colbie noticed. "Thank you, Sir . . ."

Bidding a quick goodbye to their server, they stepped through the front door onto the sidewalk, both lost in their own thoughts. "So," Decklin asked as Colbie plucked her cell from her messenger bag, then tapped the screen, signaling Anderson to pick her up. "Where do we go from here?"

"I'm hoping you'll agree—I'd like you to ramp up a thorough investigation on Carmen Santosa."

"Easy to do—we already have the list of Hector's patients, so it won't be unusual for us to inquire about someone on it."

"I won't ask how you achieved such a thing—but, I'm impressed!" Colbie glanced to her left, expecting Anderson to appear any moment. "Again, well done!"

"I appreciate the accolades—and, to answer your question, Analena Cortina gave it to us."

A quick glance at an approaching vehicle. "Let's talk later. My chariot is here . . ."

So, with that, Colbie Colleen and Decklin Kilgarry parted, both knowing their case was amping up. There was, however, a great deal they still needed to learn—more than they knew. As she bade him goodbye, Decklin noticed her vehicle changed from a black SUV to a white, nondescript make and model. Not a surprise, really, but the change did serve to solidify the importance of their assignment.

That was good.

Colbie nodded to Anderson as she climbed into the back seat of the SUV, her mind on one thing. "The beach location," she directed, knowing she didn't need to say more.

Without turning to look at her, Anderson pulled away from the curb, then asked his question. "Who are we meeting this late?"

"Gisele."

"Isn't that a little risky?"

"Unfortunately, we have no choice—Gisele has newly acquired information, and she indicated time is a factor."

Saying nothing more, Anderson turned onto the freeway heading south, recognizing the urgency in Colbie's voice—something he rarely heard. From the time he was assigned to work as her driver, she rarely displayed anything but calm. "Five minutes out," he informed her as he turned onto a dark road leading to a lonely beach.

"I'll be back in ten," Colbie advised as soon as Anderson parked, then scanned the area making sure no one was around. "If I'm not, you know what to do . . ."

Swell, Anderson thought as he watched her disappear down a well-hidden, sandy path leading to a single bench close to the water. He knew the dangers of their current assignment, and things were beginning to get dicey. If things went belly up?

A bad situation.

Not glancing at Colbie as she sat down, Gisele kept her eyes on the ebb and flow of the water's edge. "Thank you for meeting me . . ."

"Not a problem—what have you learned?"

"A lot. There's a change coming, but I don't know how soon—operations will change within the Mexican cartel."

Colbie's eyebrows shot north, realizing Gisele acquired new information—something their assignment needed. "How do you know?"

"Juan Fuentes popped a surprise visit on Aidan—and, at first, he wasn't too thrilled about it."

"What did Fuentes want?"

Suddenly, Gisele turned to Colbie, her eyes dark and serious. "He advised Aidan he has a short time to live—and, from the way he looked, his time isn't far off. It's because of that, he's turned over the reins to his daughter . . ."

"Gloria?"

A nod.

"Why did Fuentes need to tell Aidan?" Colbie had her suspicions, of course, but it was always better to hear it from the proverbial horse's mouth.

"Because Fuentes wanted and needed to be certain nothing interrupted their current business arrangement." Then, Gisele reached into her dress pocket, producing a thumb drive. "For you . . ."

Taking the drive, Colbie sat back on the bench, smiling, playing the part of a dear friend, knowing she had three minutes before ending their surreptitious meeting. To anyone interested, she and Gisele were like everyone else in South Beach doing their own thing in their own time.

So, precisely ten minutes after she arrived, Colbie Colleen bid Gisele goodbye, turning to wave before heading up the sandy trail.

Mission accomplished.

CHAPTER 13

*A*gain, Decklin checked the list of Hector Cortina's patients, wondering if there were someone else they needed to consider in addition to Carmen Santosa.

"What about the Social Hour group," Devon asked as he, too, reviewed the list. "What's going on with that?"

"You mean who other than Tom Sandoval has a dog in the fight?" Decklin paused as he jotted down a name. "Well, the only other person who's involved is Aidan Lopez—maybe. When Colbie and I talked about it, she said they suspected his involvement, but couldn't get proof—that's Gisele Escalante's job. When Colbie attended the Social Hour gathering with Sandoval, Lopez gave her nothing other than a few laughs. He was the perfect host, refusing to talk about business . . ."

"Well, why don't I do a little digging," Devon suggested, knowing his partner had enough on his plate.

"Exactly my thought—Colbie mentioned they hadn't thoroughly researched Aidan's father."

"Why's he important?"

"Because he turned the company over to his son before passing several years ago—and, I suspect the father's expectation was Aidan's operating the shipping business exactly the way he did. That means, of course, same clients, same favors . . ."

Devon smiled, understanding where Decklin was headed. "Okay—I'll dive into both. What about you?"

"Carmen Santosa—from prelim work, I'm convinced she's a shadow presence on the Internet. If she has anything to do with intel being passed from her homeland, staying off of social media is a good idea. Here's a photo . . ."

"Well, she can't be stupid to hold the job she has— maybe she posts on social media under a fake name." Devon slid the picture of Carmen Santosa closer to him, squinting as he committed it to memory. "Of course, she could be a woman who simply wanted to change her image—but, there's something about her I don't trust."

A nod. "I agree."

So, clear on their respective investigation duties, Decklin and Devon went their own ways, agreeing to keep in touch via text until the next time both were in the office. "Let's give it a week to see what we can dig up . . ."

As it turned out, it was a good thing Juan Fuentes took care of business when he did—two weeks after meeting with Aidan Lopez, funeral arrangements were underway, Juan's wife and daughters planning a huge send-off. Of course, Aidan attended, but only because of his impeccable good taste—to not make an appearance? Obvious repercussions. A few days later?

Back to business.

First on his list of things to do was task Gisele with contacting clients who were close to Juan Fuentes to assure them there would be no interruption in business. He also appointed her the go-to person for any questions or complaints—something he felt wasn't in his job description. Besides, Gisele was good at her job, and there was no reason to think she wouldn't rise to the occasion. The only drawback?

She may be perceived as a replacement for Aidan.

Understanding her new assignments, the first thing Gisele needed to do was cement the positive business relationship with the new Mexican mafia queen. "Gloria! Thank you for meeting me on such short notice—it's rare I have a break in my schedule, and I wanted to be sure we touch base!"

The obligatory hug.

"And, thank you for attending my father's services," Gloria responded, a tiny catch in her voice—but, while it was a nice touch, Gisele wasn't buying any of it. Though she had few occasions to be in the same room with the newly-appointed cartel leader, as soon as Gloria walked into her office, she displayed an air of confidence and a Kevlar exterior. "I appreciate the opportunity to meet—we have much to discuss," Gloria began as she took a seat at a small table in Gisele's office. Eyeing the plate of appetizers and sparkling water, she chose an appetizer, popping it in her mouth before Gisele had a chance to sit down. A tell?

Oh, yes.

"Agreed—as sad as your father's passing is, I suspect you'll lead your organization in accordance with his wishes. But, I also know you'll bring your own style . . ." Scrutinizing Gloria, Gisele smiled to herself—the fact Gloria met Gisele on her home turf displayed a certain weakness, and Gloria was oblivious.

"You're right—my father served our organization always demanding respect. But, over the years, it became apparent his business relationships should be revamped—and, that's what I intend to do."

"Including Allied International Shipping?"

Gloria smiled before jamming another appetizer in her mouth. "Of course—that's why I'm here!" Displaying a slight glare as she chewed, she kept her focus on the woman across from her. In her mind, she was merely taking charge—in Gisele's mind, however?

Gloria Fuentes was trouble.

"So, what is it you think we need to change," Gisele asked, forcing her voice to remain calm.

"Well, you have to admit, Aidan is faltering somewhat when it comes to our trade agreement, especially with Cuba and the Far East."

"Faltering? As far as I know, we've increased our routes, always meeting changing expectations."

"Well, perhaps—but, my new goal for our organization is much greater than in the past, and I'm uncertain whether Allied International Shipping will be capable of keeping up."

An insult Gisele didn't take kindly.

"Where would you like us to focus our attention," she finally asked not taking her eyes from Gloria's.

"First, we need to bump up international traffic—we're missing opportunities, especially with the whole southern border situation." A moment to think. "And, COVID created a chaos we appreciate, also increasing possibilities."

"I understand. So, let me ask you—are you capable of providing enough product to make the shipping profitable?" Yes, it was a nasty little question, but one Gisele couldn't resist.

Target acquired.

"We will provide the product—but, I must have assurances your international shipping will include all countries on my list." Gloria reached into her handbag, producing a small piece of paper. "Our clients must always receive their first shipment within two weeks—are you certain you can deliver?"

"Of course."

"I run a tight ship, Gisele—I hope you do, too." With that, Gloria Fuentes stood, grabbing another appetizer. "One for the road," she laughed as she headed for the door.

Gisele smiled, saying nothing since Gloria didn't expect a response. Moments later, she was out the door, leaving the top operations expert of Allied International Shipping to her thoughts.

And, they weren't good.

Through binos, Devon eyed brightly colored shipping containers, as well as workers on the docks, targeting who may be more inclined to have loose lips. It was a crapshoot, of course, but, if he had to put money on it, two guys standing in a sliver of shade provided by one of the massive ships seemed a reasonable bet.

Accessing them, however, could be a problem.

Sensing his time for conversation with them would be short, he locked his car, then headed for the closest dock. Scanning the area as he approached, the men eyed him, ceasing all conversation as Devon reached earshot. "Good afternoon, Gentlemen," he called, a huge smile plastered on his face. "I'm wondering if you can answer a question—I'm doing research on international commerce, and I figure going to the source is a good idea!"

Too bad both men barely spoke English.

Instantly recognizing the language barrier, Devon dragged out his Spanish, pleased he could speak it fluently thanks to the benefits of being a rich kid.

That was all it took.

Both men smiled broadly, accepted Devon's offered hand, then invited him into the shade. "Look, I don't want to take up your time," Devon began, "because I know you're on the clock—but, what can you tell me about working on the docks? Do you enjoy it? Are you paid fairly?"

Laughing, both longshoremen shook their heads. "Not enough," both advised. "We haven't had a raise in three years," the taller man confided, "but, what are we going to do? No one listens . . ."

As Devon listened, he realized both men were overworked and underpaid. "But, what about your union—doesn't it fight for you?"

"Some," the shorter man commented. "But, it's not enough—and, if we say anything." A pause. "Well . . ."

Briefly scanning the ships in port, Devon again turned to the men. "What's in the containers," he asked, hoping for a specific answer.

Again, the shorter longshoreman took the lead with a shrug. "We don't know . . ."

"Anything unusual?"

Another shrug. "Sometimes, we hear sounds . . ."

"Sounds? What kind of sounds?"

Glancing at each other, the men informed Devon they had to get back to work, dismissing him as they headed for the massive lot of shipping containers.

At least I got something, he thought as he headed back to his car. Suddenly, he turned, checking out each direction as a shudder darted up his spine. Seeing no one, he continued to his vehicle, the uncomfortable feeling gaining strength. Again, as he unlocked his car, he scanned the parking lot and the docks. *Nothing . . .*

But, there was something.

Gloria Fuentes's top man trained his binos on the young man driving a fancy car, the man's intuition in full gear. Keeping the binos on his target, he reached for his cell with one hand, briefly lowering them to connect his call, then returned to his surveillance. "Something ain't right," he informed his contact in Spanish. "Tell the boss . . ."

As it turned out, Carmen Santosa proved to be a bit of a problem—with little information about her on the Internet, Decklin had to get creative when it came to securing information they could use. Still, he wasn't sure if it would be enough.

Knowing she was educated in Cuba then the United States, the only thing he could find was a photo of her college graduation and, from what he could tell, Santosa barely resembled the photo Colbie shared with him. Tall and slender, short, dark hair gave her a rather chiseled look, an elegance Decklin appreciated. *I can't believe this is the same woman . . .*

It was, though.

Granted, the photo was taken nearly twenty years prior, but there was no mistaking the amount of work Hector Cortina performed on Santosa, attempting to craft the perfect face. Gone was the natural elegance, replaced by something unpleasant—something hard. *What if Santosa altered her appearance for reasons other than vanity,* he suddenly considered, the thought making sense. *If that's the case, what does she have to hide?*

And, that was the question, wasn't it?

Until then, Decklin hadn't considered a possible ulterior motive as powerful motivation for Carmen's cosmetic surgery, but it certainly could be so.

As much as he didn't want to use contacts from his time as a D.C. detective, the situation warranted obtaining obscure information. With that in mind, within a few hours Decklin had information he needed, knowing what he discovered might help their overall cause. As it turned out?

Carmen Santosa was the daughter of a Cuban diplomat who never shied away from the regime's wants and needs.

Always a proponent of her father's political leanings, Carmen grew up in his shadow until she emigrated to the U.S.—something piquing Decklin's interest. *If her father were respected in Cuba,* he wondered, *why the hell would she give up the good life to come to the States?* The more Decklin thought about it, the more Carmen Santosa was becoming an enigma.

But, there was more—after arriving in the U.S., she attended a prestigious university without taking a student loan for her education and, in Decklin's mind, that meant she got tuition money from somewhere.

Or, someone with a vested interest.

Time to introduce myself to Amelia Sandoval, Decklin thought after concluding his initial research on Carmen Santosa. Tossing notes in his desk drawer then turning the key, there was little doubt she was a connecting thread in their investigation. As much as Decklin didn't enjoy stepping on Devon's toes, the time had come for experience to prevail— but, not before talking to his partner and Analena Cortina.

Without bothering to text first, Decklin tapped in Analena's number, hoping to reach her on the first try so he could ask a few questions. That day?

The gods were with him.

"I've been going over the list of Hector's patients, and there's one I'm hoping you can shed light on—Carmen Santosa," Decklin began, still unsure if Analena would answer.

"Carmen? I don't really know her, but I did meet her on a couple of occasions . . ."

"What type of occasion—and, when did you last see her?"

"I saw her several weeks ago at a Cuban culture festival, but not since then." Analena paused, trying to recall seeing Hector's patient more than once within the last six months. "As I said, Mr. Kilgarry, she's not even an acquaintance— and, I have no reason to change that since she's the one who filed a lawsuit against my husband."

"I understand—and, I apologize for my next question, Analena, but did Hector have a special interest in Carmen?"

"Maybe."

"Why do you think so?"

"I don't—I simply think it's possible Hector had an interest in many of his patients." A quiet moment before Analena divulged exactly what she thought of her husband. "My husband is a liar, Mr. Kilgarry—and, it's because of that I realize I will probably never know the truth about his life."

"Are there other truths you know about other than his infidelities?"

Another silence. "Other than his lying about the lawsuits filed against him for unacceptable work?"

"Yes—do you think Hector is involved in anything illegal?"

Again, Analena was quiet as if weighing the possible consequences regarding her life if she spoke what she believed to be true. "No."

As Decklin listened, he knew she was lying, but her next words stunned him to the core. "I'll be filing for divorce, Mr. Kilgarry—so, I no longer need your services. I realize who my husband truly is, and I have no desire to continue a relationship with him."

"Are you—"

"Yes—I'm sure. I appreciate your efforts, but, as I said, I no longer need to learn anything about Hector."

Honoring her request, Decklin ended the call, knowing he shouldn't have been surprised. All Analena wanted to learn was why her husband was hauled off to the clink— and, in the beginning, that was the only thing. As Decklin's case bloomed, however, it became clear Hector was living a lie when it came to fidelity, and Decklin could only imagine the hurt in Analena's heart. *What else is he lying about,* he wondered as he tapped in Devon's number on speed dial.

As soon as Devon answered, Decklin delivered the news, advising him to continue his deep dive into Aidan Lopez and his father. "When you think about it," Decklin commented, "we haven't been on the same trajectory since we learned Hector was arrested because of the bench warrants—and, that's been some time ago. I don't blame Analena for firing us—as far as she's concerned, we did our job."

"Are you going to let Colbie know?"

"Well, I hadn't thought about that, but I should—after all, Analena was a contact for us and, unfortunately, that dried up."

So, with that in mind, Decklin knew his next call needed to be to Colbie Colleen, clear there was a possibility she could end his and Devon's involvement in their investigation should she feel they were no longer needed.

All he could do was hope that wasn't the case.

CHAPTER 14

"Thanks for letting me know," Colbie responded, "but I see no reason to discontinue our working arrangement. I doubt Analena Cortina knows anything about her husband's suspected duplicity—and, even if she did, she may not care."

"Excellent—I feel we're only seeing the tip of the iceberg regarding Hector's possible treason and, in a way, it's time to weed out those who don't make a difference."

"I agree—and, Analena's one of them."

With Decklin's apprehension laid to rest, Colbie wasted no time to discuss what Decklin learned since they last met. "When considering Carmen Santosa," he began, "she leaves me with a bad taste in my mouth. Though I have no proof, I have little doubt she's involved simply because she's in a perfect position for it."

"Yes, but she's also exceedingly careful. In fact, if it hadn't been for rummaging through discarded trash, we'd never know the truth—and, what we learned wasn't much."

"The suspected truth," Decklin corrected. "Analena mentioned she saw Carmen at a Cuban festival a few weeks ago, so that makes me think she might attend the next one, too—and, that's in a couple of weeks."

"A perfect time to see what she's up to, don't you think?"

"Not to mention it's a perfect way to pass information to her contact . . ."

"Hector?"

"Or, someone else . . ."

With that, both clicked off, Decklin redirecting his efforts to something more important than missed bench warrants. If Hector Cortina were a traitor to his country, it was time to show him a cell block door. If not?

Back to the drawing board.

"What did you learn about Aidan Lopez," Decklin asked as Devon sat across from him on a bench provided by a local food truck. "Anything new?"

Devon took a bite of his chicken taco, then swiped at his mouth with a napkin. "Yep—especially when considering international shipping opens up the world for illegal business."

Decklin opened two packets of ranch dressing, then emptied both onto his tacos. "Agreed. So, what do we know?"

A disbelieving stare. "Are you kidding me? Ranch dressing on a taco? That's sacrilege!"

"Can't do the hot stuff—my stomach can't take it."

"I'm surprised they even have ranch dressing . . ."

"Only in America—it's everywhere!" Assessing his tacos, Decklin dove in, soon reaching for a napkin, but not until he mugged for his partner. "Do I have something on my face?"

Shaking his head and with a gut laugh, Devon tossed another napkin to him. "Nope—not a damned thing!"

As they ate, Decklin realized Devon was really the only person he knew in South Beach—well, other than Colbie, but that didn't really count. After bringing her case to fruition, she, undoubtedly, would be off to somewhere else, leaving Decklin to his memories.

A rather solemn realization.

"So, tell me . . ."

Taking a drink of his iced tea, Devon chased it with another bite. "Gilberto Lopez was an interesting man, playing an important role in international shipping—and, he had a stellar reputation? until he was suspected of trafficking drugs a couple of decades ago. Nothing ever came of it, however, and it soon was no longer news."

"Why weren't there charges brought against him?"

"Good question—no prosecutable proof, I guess." Devon glanced at a couple walking by their picnic bench, lowering his voice slightly. "It's how Aidan's father lived his life that's more interesting to me . . ."

"Meaning?"

"Quite the ladies man, and there was never a time when he showed up at an event without a beautiful woman on his arm."

"What about Aidan's mother—Gilberto's wife?"

"Never in the picture—but, there wasn't a divorce, so perhaps she agreed to stay out of the limelight."

"Maybe—there also could've been an unspoken arrangement between the two. I'm guessing they lived an influential and extravagant lifestyle, and maybe it was more important than love lost between them."

An interesting perspective.

It wouldn't be the first time a couple stayed married because of financial perks and, if that were the case, Aidan's mother probably wouldn't have knowledge about the true inner workings of her husband's company. Why would she? If living in luxury's lap, kicking her lifestyle to the curb could be a tough thing to do. "Okay," Decklin continued, "what else do you have?"

"Well, I paid a visit to the Miami docks—you know, just to see how things worked. How people looked while doing their jobs . . ."

"Did you learn anything?"

"Yep—and, the two most important things, I think, deserve our attention." Before launching into what he learned at the shipyard, Devon finished his taco, then tossed the to-go container into the trash. "When I got there, I was lucky enough to snag a parking space with a view of the docks—and, two men talking. My guess is they were on break . . ."

"Probably union."

"That's right—so, after watching the shipyard for a few minutes, I decided to take a chance. I wanted to ask the two guys a few questions, so they were my target."

"They talked to you?"

"A little—they didn't speak English well, so I dipped into what Spanish I knew, asking them if they liked working there."

"What did they say?"

"They shrugged their shoulders, but did say they weren't paid enough, and they haven't had a raise for the last three years. When I asked if their union fought for them, it was another shoulder shrug." Another sip of iced tea. "But, it was what they said next that interested me—when I asked what were in the containers, they didn't say much. The one guy, though, said they sometimes hear sounds coming from inside the containers, but they refused to elaborate when I pressed them on it, and that's when they left."

Finishing his tacos, Decklin, too, tossed his to-go container into the trash. "I agree—that does raise questions. When people don't want to talk about things they know, avoidance is a good tactic. So, that makes me wonder if they know what's in those containers—did they elaborate on what kind of sounds?"

Devon shook his head. "Nope—and, when I asked, it was pretty clear they didn't want to be involved."

For the next few minutes, Decklin and Devon tossed around viable ideas, neither coming to a conclusion. With that topic tabled, it was time to turn to other things. "I think it's time I have a conversation with Amelia Sandoval," Decklin suggested. "I have a feeling she knows much more about what's going on than she leads us to believe . . ."

"Agreed."

By the time Decklin turned the key in his condo's door, an unpleasant weight took root, convincing him he needed to put his cases aside for an evening. Throwing his keys on the foyer table, he kicked off his shoes, then plopped on the couch, rubbing his eyes. But, as he sat, he couldn't help think of Cecily, her voice echoing in his mind. "You don't know when to give it up," she often chastised. "You need to take care of you. Us . . ."

Advice he chose to ignore.

Once again, he allowed his work to interfere with his personal life and, once again, he opted to avoid confrontation rather than fight for his relationship. That, however, was something he rarely considered, not realizing his ineptitude to deal with something uncomfortable carried a pain he chose not to endure. In fact, whenever he thought about Cecily, Decklin refused to acknowledge his skill in oft-practiced avoidance techniques. *What good does fighting do*, he often wondered, that evening no exception. *Besides, it takes two . . .*

That was true.

Shortly after moving to Miami, Cecily began to change, though she rarely discussed why, causing Decklin to wonder if she recognized it. And, that was what Decklin couldn't understand—if they were planning on spending their lives together, shouldn't she at least have let him know she was unhappy?

One would think.

Water under the bridge, he thought as he suddenly got up, snatched his keys from the foyer table, then checked his hair in the mirror, deeming himself presentable enough to attempt a conversation with Amelia Sandoval. As thoughts of Cecily receded, Decklin knew what he needed to accomplish, and chastising himself for failed relationships wouldn't do a damned thing when it came to figuring out who was playing a dangerous game in Miami. Lesson learned?

Not really.

It's always interesting to dissect misplaced motivations, especially when they involve the seamier side of life—and, if Hector Cortina would've taken a prolonged look at himself, he might've anticipated his life was about to change at the most inopportune time.

"Please, Hector—come back to bed!" Gloria Fuentes pleaded, patting the spot beside her as she struck her best seductive pose. As she told her father before his passing, if there were one thing Hector Cortina couldn't resist, it was an alluring body other than his wife's. "It seems as if we never talk anymore," she cajoled, "and, I don't want our relationship to be one of silence."

Of course, she didn't.

Was lacking communication an age-old lament in many relationships? Yes. But, Hector didn't care about such things. He thought he was clear when he took up sheets with the mafia don's daughter, not quite understanding their codes of silence were different. Well, kind of—to be accurate, Hector didn't really have a code of silence, and the only thing he wanted was to enjoy his trysts without Analena's discovering his marital duplicity.

Gloria, conversely, made it clear to all concerned that two, well-placed bullets would be the reward for discussing where she went and whom she saw. In order to achieve her goal—which was, of course, ascertaining information regarding deeply held Cuban intel—she needed to keep Hector Cortina all to herself.

"We don't talk?" Hector turned, eyeing Gloria from head to toe. "What's there to talk about?"

"Well, business . . ."

While she thought of a more acceptable answer, Hector grabbed his clothes from the side of the bed, then headed for the bathroom. "We can talk later—I have to go."

When he exited ten minutes later?

Alone in the room.

CHAPTER 15

As much as Decklin would've liked to surprise Amelia Sandoval at her front door, building security wasn't about to let anyone inside without proper I.D.—something Decklin anticipated. So, as twilight fell, all he could do was park himself far enough away from Amelia's swanky apartment building, hoping she would be going out or returning within a reasonable time.

Again alone with his thoughts, he ditched maudlin for something more constructive until his cell chirped. "What can I do for you, Ms. Colleen," his voice smiling as he pictured the petite redhead.

"What are you doing right now," she asked, leaving pleasantries on an invisible doorstep.

"Surveilling Amelia Sandoval's apartment building. I'm hoping to have an impromptu conversation with her . . ."

"About?"

"Whether her husband knew of her Santeria beliefs and affiliation—and, if she knew he worked for the U.S. government, did she compromise that situation by passing confidential information. Time for some hardball . . ."

"Sounds like a tricky conversation to me—but, I didn't call simply to check on your whereabouts." Colbie hesitated for a moment, cycling through what the next hours may hold. "I need you to abort your conversation with Amelia . . ."

"Why?"

"Hector Cortina was just found with two, well-placed bullets between the eyes."

"Damn!"

"I know—and, that bit of news puts us on a different trajectory. If Hector is—was—a main player for passing U.S. intel to the Cubans, the question becomes why was he taken out?"

"Obviously, someone was displeased with him. And, it will behoove us to know the reason why . . ."

"We know Hector met with Gloria Fuentes last evening at the Pink Palm . . ."

"A Miami hotel?"

"A glitzy one, costing plenty."

Decklin was silent for a few seconds, trying to anticipate Colbie's reason for calling. "Interesting—so, why am I calling off my surveillance on Amelia?"

"I need you to stick to Analena like glue."

"Do you think she offed her husband?"

"It's a possibility—after all, it wouldn't be the first time a woman scorned took matters into her own hands."

"I don't know—she doesn't seem like the type who has the stomach for it."

"Maybe not—if that's the case, we need to eliminate her quickly. Things are heating up, and we know Gloria is at the center of it."

As Decklin listened while keeping one eye on Amelia Sandoval's apartment building, there was little doubt Colbie was keeping something from him. Not wanting to create waves, however, he decided to let it go, knowing it would be revealed later. "Alright—does Analena know about Hector?"

"I'm assuming she does by now, but I'm not certain—local authorities are handling it. We can't afford to tip our hand, so we're keeping tabs behind the scenes."

"Understood." Decklin glanced at his watch, noting it was too late to contact Hector's wife. "I'll call her tomorrow under the auspices of terminating our contract—if she knows about Hector, my gut says she'll tell me."

"Keep me apprised." With nothing more, Colbie severed the connection, leaving Decklin to wonder who the hell wanted Hector Cortina out of the way.

And, why.

As far as Decklin and Devon interpreted the whole mess, treason had to be the root cause of everything—and, not only in the usual sense. Knowing Analena was aware of her husband's infidelity—a treasonous act in her mind—it was possible she decided enough was enough.

Decklin, however, didn't think so.

"Of course, I'll do what Colbie requests, but thinking Analena dusted her husband doesn't make sense."

Devon leaned against the frame of Decklin's office door, arms crossing his chest. "Agreed. I think taking her husband for everything he's worth is more her style. I think she'd rather have him suffer from embarrassment and poverty—it lasts longer."

"My thought exactly."

"So, if Analena didn't do it, who did?"

Decklin sat back in his desk chair, clicking the end of his pen. "The million-dollar question—and, my money's on Gloria Fuentes. At least for now . . ."

"What about Amelia Sandoval? We know she's into some pretty bizarre shit—maybe Hector was some sort of initiation or sacrifice."

"Good thought—both fit Santeria, I'm guessing, and we know for sure the mafia employs it as a rite of passage."

"True—who do we investigate first?"

"Amelia. I'll talk to Analena, of course, and I should be able to determine if she murdered Hector. While I'm doing that, you can keep eyes on Amelia. When I'm done with Analena, I'll take over . . ."

"What about after that?"

"We'll switch again—it's a sure bet Hector's body won't be released until after an autopsy, so he'll be on ice for a while. In the meantime, it'll be interesting to learn where Amelia goes and whom she sees . . ."

"On it . . ." With a smile and his usual half-salute, Devon headed out the door, thinking of his surveillance approach. Knowing Amelia and Analena were once tight friends, he could reasonably assume they had similar tastes. If he couldn't find Amelia at home, at least he had a good idea of where to look.

With two bullets smack dab between the eyes, there was little doubt Hector Cortina met his end at the hands of someone who hated his guts. Or, someone who wanted to send a message—a thought prompting Decklin to take a leisurely drive past Rossi's on a warm Sunday afternoon. Turning onto the street tucked among the palms, the nondescript restaurant didn't look any different than it did the two times he was there—until he noticed black sedans lining the side street flanking the rear of the building.

Maybe I should let Colbie know, he thought as he drove slowly by, considering the cars belonged to one of Miami's crime families. *At least it can't hurt,* he decided as he parked down the street with an unobstructed view of the restaurant's rear exit—then, he tapped his cell screen.

Busy? Time for a meeting?

"Good. That was generic enough," Decklin muttered to himself as he awaited a reply, cell in hand. Moments later, a response bloomed on his screen.

On my way. Where?

Quickly, Decklin tapped in his location, all the while keeping one eye on his target and, within twenty, Colbie arrived, joining him within the comfort of his air-conditioned car. "Okay—I'm here. What's up?"

"It may be nothing, but I don't think so . . ."

"You mean the black cars? Pretty conspicuous, don't you think?"

"So, you know they're cartel?"

A nod. "Yep—or, mafia. Same thing, really, and it's no secret Miami's been controlled by the Cuban mafia for decades. Ever since Reagan effectively handed them the keys to the city in the '80s."

"Seriously?"

"Oh, yes—but, that's a discussion for another time. Now, however, we know at least one more location for their meetings. Never taking her eyes from Rossi's back door,

Colbie figured it was time to elucidate. "Today's Miami Cubans hail from a corrupt partnership between the Batista government and the mob—and, throughout the decades, many Miami Cubans are living as U.S. citizens. All the while, they've rewritten history, effectively creating their dream Havana outside of their native country."

"You're sure the cars belong to the Miami mafia?"

Another nod. "Pretty sure—it's how they do things in New Jersey."

"New Jersey? What the hell does New Jersey have to do with anything?" Decklin glanced at Colbie, but only for a moment as he tried to process what she just said.

"Just this—as you know, Fidel Castro ousted Fulgencio Batista who was in lockstep with the mob." Colbie paused, watching a restaurant employee step outside for a smoke. "That, obviously, was in the 1950s and early '60s."

"Okay. I still don't . . ."

"I don't blame you for being a little confused—I was until I began putting two and two together." Colbie smiled at her new colleague. "So, that led to the Brigade 2506 . . ."

"Which is?"

"The Brigade 2506—formed in 1960—was a CIA-sponsored group of Cuban exiles designated to attempt a military coup against the Cuban government which, as you know, was led by Castro. It has to do with the Bay of Pigs in 1961, plus other stuff—but, for now, all you need to know about is Jose Miguel Battle, who was a former Batista policeman. After members of the Brigade 2506 were released from incarceration—"

"They were jailed," Decklin asked, trying to make sense of what Colbie was telling him.

"Oh, yes—Castro didn't take kindly to their failed attempt at a governmental overthrow, and the first thing he did was slam a few of them in jail." Colbie again paused, pointing to a man exiting the back door of the restaurant, then climb into one of the shiny, black sedans.

"Do you want to follow," Decklin asked, unsure of how she wanted to proceed.

Colbie shook her head slightly. "No—we know they have meetings, but this is the first time we've seen them be so flagrant regarding their location." She paused as another man exited the restaurant, then headed toward one of the new vehicles. "So, to continue—when those guys got out of jail, some of the Brigade members formed an organization known as The Corporation."

"What was the main business of The Corporation," Decklin asked, though he was certain of Colbie's response.

"It was a Cuban American criminal organization that worked directly with the Italian mafia—so, you can imagine the money that was changing hands. Gambling, drug trafficking, and a bunch of other usual mob stuff laced their pockets. Murder, too . . ."

"So, if Battle were from New Jersey, how did his group wind up in Miami?"

"Simple—it was about location and money. The Corporation's money was coupled with CIA funds, as well as money obtained from CIA-trained Cubans involved in the illicit drug business. They helped with incursions into Cuba, attempting to take down Castro's government."

Decklin was quiet, digesting everything. "So," he finally commented, "obviously they became the Miami mafia . . ."

"Exactly—it really was the beginning of the Miami mafia. And, right from the start, anyone showing an interest in going against their ways was intimidated—they lost jobs and, sometimes, their lives. Those who disagreed were held hostage—figuratively, of course."

"Interesting—especially since we usually think of the mafia as being Italian."

"I know—but, when you look up the word 'mafia?' It's any of various similar criminal organizations, especially when dominated by members of the same nationality."

"So, the Mexican mafia is still alive and well in Miami—and, Gloria Fuentes is now their leader."

A nod. "Yep—the Miami mafia. And, make no mistake—she's as brutal and ruthless as her father with little caring for the human condition. As long as there's money to be made by extortion and trafficking, she's in on the deal—a chip off the old block, yet more cold-blooded and malevolent."

Again, Decklin was quiet as he cycled through Colbie's information. "Do you think she took out Hector Cortina?"

"Not personally—Gloria's not one to get her fingernails dirty with such trivial nonsense. But, it's a sure bet she hired one of her men to do the deed if, in fact, she's to blame."

"But, you do think it was the Miami Mafia . . ."

"If I were a betting woman? I'd take those odds . . ."

So, for the next thirty or so minutes, Decklin and Colbie sat in his car, watching as men dressed in black exited through the restaurant's back door, each claiming one of the black vehicles.

"During one of my conversations with Analena," Decklin offered seconds before Colbie called their surveillance quits, "she intimated her husband could've been involved in illegal stuff—but, she didn't know for certain. It could, however, be the reason Hector left her during the night, never returning until the following day . . ."

"That," Colbie said with a smile, "I'd bet on . . ."

CHAPTER 16

*A*s expected, news of Hector's taking two bullets to the brain topped most news stories, especially in Little Havana and Miami. Stunned by her husband's murder, Analena requested privacy for her and her family and much of the press complied, leaving more questions on reporter's lips. If they ever learned the truth, it would undoubtedly be juicy, and more than one investigative journalist was salivating at the mere thought.

Decklin, however, had other things on his mind.

Taking a brazen chance, he arrived at Analena's home, hoping to offer condolences coupled with underlying motives. Fully aware speaking with her would be iffy, he rang the doorbell, its sound reverberating throughout a massive foyer. Moments later, a man opened the door, shooting Decklin the stink eye. "I thought Mrs. Cortina was clear—no interviews."

"I'm not with the press, Sir—my name is Decklin Kilgarry, and I'm Analena's private investigator."

Not quite true, but true enough.

"Wait here." Leaving Decklin on the veranda, the man closed the door, then returned a few minutes later. "Mrs. Cortina will see you," he advised, gesturing for Decklin to step inside as he opened the door.

Crossing the threshold, Decklin scanned the expansive space, jotting mental notes. Paintings lined the wall, some by famous artists, others not so much. Decorated with a Cuban flair, there was no mistaking the couple's preference regarding interior design. Modern, bold prints were paired flawlessly with sleek furnishings, each space claiming its own, subtle communication.

"Come with me," the man directed, leading Decklin to a small room off the main hallway. "Please sit—Mrs. Cortina will be with you shortly."

Decklin watched him go, wondering what position he held within the family dynamic. *Probably a butler*, he thought as he listened to high heels clicking on the white, marble floor—then, a voice to go with them. "Hello, Mr. Kilgarry . . ."

Decklin rose, offering his hand and condolences. "I'm sorry to hear . . ."

Analena sat across from Decklin, offering a rare opportunity to notice the lines of life etching her face.

"Thank you—it's difficult."

"Of course, it is—I'm sure you have a million questions about Hector's murder, but it's sometimes hard to recognize whom you can trust—and, I'm here to let you know you can trust me."

Silence.

"I can help find out who attempted to destroy your family and, now that I'm sitting across from you, I see your resolve is iron clad." A pause as he tried to read her expression. "You're a strong woman, Analena, and I know you'll rise above all of it."

Well, that was all Analena Cortina needed to hear.

Straightening slightly and with tight lips, rising to the occasion suited her. "You're correct, Mr. Kilgarry—I am strong. My family is strong . . ." Analena hesitated as if mentally grasping for something important. "I want to find out who murdered my husband," she continued, "and, when, I do, it will be that person's darkest day." A mistakenly spoken truth?

Yep.

"How can I help," Decklin asked, knowing her answer might not be one he wanted to hear.

"Find him—then, bring him to me." A dictum? Maybe. But, either way, it was an order Decklin didn't appreciate. He leaned forward, clasping his hands. "How about this— I'll find him, then turn him over to the authorities."

Apparently, Analena Cortina had to think about it, creating a whole new image of her in Decklin's mind. Clearly, she was comfortable ordering people to do her bidding and, at that moment, she expected her ex-private investigator to do the same.

Wasn't gonna happen.

Sitting back in his chair, Decklin continued as if the woman across from him already gave her consent. "You and I have a bit of a history, Analena—we've discussed the fact you didn't trust your husband. Other things, too—one of which was his leaving in the middle of the night, not returning until the following day." A moment's silence. "Do you recall?"

"Yes—and, as I said before, Hector's leaving in the middle of the night had nothing to do with seeing another woman. If it were that, I'd know—a woman's intuition, I think."

"What do you think now?"

"I suspect Hector was meeting someone—but, not for personal needs. Something else . . ."

"Do you have any idea regarding why Hector was meeting someone?"

"No—but, knowing Hector, it could be anything."

"Drugs?"

"Oh, no! Hector would never do anything so low class— no, I think it was something paying him a lot of money without getting his hands dirty. Something dark in the dark, if you know what I mean."

Decklin took a second to figure out how to phrase his next question, ultimately deciding on the direct approach. "We also talked about Carmen Santosa—and, I'm thinking they were directly linked."

It was an interesting approach—kind of a quid pro quo thing. If he were honest about certain things with Analena, she may be more comfortable relaying pertinent information in return.

Worth a shot, anyway.

"I agree with you—but, Carmen Santosa isn't the type of woman my husband would be interested in, Mr. Kilgarry. That alone makes me think something else was going on . . ."

"Then, if you agree, why don't I start there?" A pause with a smile. "And, just so you know, I didn't come here to get my job back. I suspect we've only scratched the surface when it comes to Hector's life—and, I admire you for being willing to explore."

Of course, Analena didn't return the smile—her heart was too heavy with reality. She did, however, offer Decklin her hand as she stood. "Do what you can, Mr. Kilgarry . . ."

So, with that, Decklin bade goodbye to his on-again client, stepping into the Florida sunlight with greater resolve than he had going in. *I'm going to find who offed Hector Cortina if it's the last damned thing I do . . .*

Promise made, promise kept.

Competition?

The nemesis of many for it brings out the worst in those who require fame and fortune to complete their lives. Knowing that, as Decklin was stuck in traffic after leaving Analena's home during rush hour, he had plenty of time to consider possibilities—and, there was one name consistently at the forefront of his investigative mind.

Thomas Sandoval.

Without knowing Sandoval personally, Decklin had the sense he wasn't everything he was cracked up to be—informant status included. Though he couldn't pinpoint where Sandoval's story diverted, Decklin still had a sense of a lacking truth.

One illuminating Thomas Sandoval's arrogance and self-serving attitude.

The only reason he was between the sheets with the U.S. government in the first place was his desire to rub elbows with Miami's socially elite. Hailing from a middle-class background, by the time he hit med school, money was calling his name. Before that?

Just a guy trying to make his way through life.

Of course, Sandoval wasn't a suspect in poor Hector's murder, but their personal and working relationships could, possibly, point to something interesting—such as Amelia Sandoval's short-lived, torrid affair with Hector. *An unlikely union*, Decklin thought as he inched forward in traffic. *And, it would be nice to know if Amelia sneaked away during the wee hours to conduct unknown business, as well . . .* A thought with untold possibilities. Another name Decklin couldn't shake?

Gloria Fuentes.

After what Colbie told him as they were parked fifty yards from Rossi's, Gloria might have had the most to gain. *Was Hector involved in cartel activities*, Decklin wondered as traffic cleared its choke hold on Miami drivers. *If so, that's a hell of a lot different than treason. Or, it could be both . . .*

In fact, the more Decklin thought about it, the more he questioned why someone like Gloria Fuentes would be interested in someone like Hector. To Decklin?

An obvious disconnect.

So, as he finally pulled into his condo parking garage, upcoming days were set with surveillance and interviews of people who probably wouldn't give him the time of day.

Still, he had to try.

Though those close to their boss knew the truth prior to Juan Fuentes's passing, few chose to acknowledge it unless they were behind closed doors.

Gloria Fuentes had a point to prove.

As with any organization, cartel success depended upon effort placed—and, according to those privy to the inner workings of the Fuentes empire, a few of Juan's top men weren't too happy with their boss's replacement. So, when word rounded toward home that Hector Cortina met his maker, those in the know had to consider it was at the hand of Juan's daughter—but, none knew for certain.

Something that was just fine with her.

Finally, the young mafia queen achieved her childhood goal of top dog within the cartel, and there was nothing anyone could do about it, except take her out of the equation.

As far as she knew? No one had the guts to do it. Besides, to accomplish such a thing took planning, and there was no way Gloria wouldn't get wind of it. Granted, she hadn't been in her queen shoes long enough to barely get her feet wet, but she wasn't an idiot. For a cartel member—or, anyone else—planning a coup, consequences would be dire. The question was would it be worth it? Probably not. On that alone, Gloria knew her position was safe . . .

New blood, new money.

CHAPTER 17

"Time to switch targets," Decklin advised when he and Devon finally got time to meet at the office. "After talking to Analena Cortina, I need to turn my attention to Amelia Sandoval . . ."

"Agreed. I didn't get too far—before Hector's murder was announced, she went the usual places. After Hector's murder? No trace . . ."

"Interesting—though, I suppose it would be in poor taste to enjoy the finer things when your friend's husband was just double tapped." A comment indicating Decklin Kilgarry was a man of class and decorum. "So, since my initial conversation was waylaid when Colbie called a few weeks ago, it's time Mrs. Sandoval and I had a little chat . . ."

"About anything in particular," Devon asked.

Decklin nodded, then withdrew his working file folder from his locked desk drawer. "Her husband—something doesn't track, and we need to know if the disconnect is because of her or him."

"Don't forget Amelia was part of the Santeria ritual—and, as we talked about before, we need to know if he knew about her preferences."

"No way he didn't—I'm sure of it. The question is was he a part of it, or did he merely tolerate it?"

Devon was quiet for a moment, thinking of something different. "Another question? Why did Thomas Sandoval embed in Miami at the behest of our government? Why him? Why not someone else?"

Decklin agreed, realizing his thoughts were echoed by his partner. "Exactly what I'm thinking—so, as of now, we switch. You're on Analena—see where she goes and who she sees. Pay particular attention to the way she looks . . ."

"You mean how she's dressed?"

"No—how she seems. You know—does she appear stressed, or is she having a grand old time now that Hector's out of the picture."

Devon headed for the door, then turned. "What about Gloria Fuentes? How are we going to get close enough to observe anything?"

"I haven't worked that out yet," Decklin admitted, tossing his pen on his desk.

"Carmen Santosa?"

"Don't you have someplace to be," Decklin asked, smiling. "You're making me look bad . . ."

As it turned out, Amelia Sandoval wasn't quite as welcoming as her friend. But, after Decklin's suggesting she contact Analena to verify he was working for her, begrudgingly, Amelia allowed entry into the building. "Thank you for seeing me," he began after she offered him a seat on her designer couch.

But, Amelia wasn't interested in pleasantries.

Perhaps it was because she lost her own husband only months prior, and she didn't want to speak to anyone, especially the press. Or, it could've been she was more unpleasant than initially thought—either way, Decklin wasn't greeted with a smile. "What can I do for you," Mr. Kilgarry," she asked as she checked her watch. "My time is limited . . ."

The Decklin Kilgarry smile. "So, is mine—so, I'll get right to it." A brief pause. "Do you know who murdered your husband and Hector Cortina?"

Amelia pulled back slightly, stunned someone would have the audacity to ask such a question, her response duly noted. "How should I know such a thing, Mr. Kilgarry?"

Interesting her answer wasn't no.

"I don't mean to insult you, Mrs. Sandoval, but you have to admit the murders of two, prominent cosmetic surgeons lend themselves to questions needing answers. If your answer is no, we'll move on . . ."

"Of course, I don't . . ."

"Okay! Moving on—do you have suspicions regarding your husband's murder? Or, Hector's?"

Amelia shook her head. "How anyone could do such a thing, I have no idea! All I have is an ankle!" A pause. "No matter what he may have done, my husband didn't deserve to be butchered!"

It was then resolve settled into Amelia Sandoval's soul.

Before Decklin could ask another question, she stood, crossing to the massive window overlooking the ocean. "But, I realize you're not here to speak of my husband," she stated as she stared out the window. "And, to answer your question, I have no idea who would want to harm Hector—he was a kind, warm, loving man."

"I'm sure he appreciated you think so highly of him . . ."

Amelia turned, arms crossed. "I said he 'was' all of those things."

"Meaning?"

"Hector Cortina changed over the last year, becoming someone few of us in his circle recognized."

"Do you mean the Social Hour circle?"

Amelia's eyebrows arched. "Yes, among a few others."

"How did he change?"

"Of course, most of my knowledge is based on what Analena told me . . ."

"I understand—what did she say?"

Amelia hesitated, as if she were debating whether to divulge confidences. "About a year ago, Analena mentioned Hector would leave in the middle of the night—something a loving husband wouldn't do."

"Why do you think he did that?"

"I can only think he was meeting someone—but, I don't think it was a woman."

"Why?"

"Because before Thomas died, he mentioned something was off with Hector."

"Did he say what?"

Amelia shook her head. "No—but, he did tell me he thought it was something illegal. Why he thought that, I don't know."

Change of course.

"Honestly, I don't know much about your husband, Mrs. Sandoval, but I do know Thomas and Hector were colleagues—is that right?"

A nod.

"Did they think highly of each other," Decklin asked, keeping his attention on her.

"My husband rarely thought highly of anyone, Mr. Kilgarry," Amelia confided, focusing on the floor.

"Including you," Decklin asked gently. "Are you speaking from experience?"

Amelia nodded, then pressed her index fingers against her eyes, hoping to stave new tears. "I always felt as if I weren't good enough for him . . ."

Without pursuing more, Decklin understood Amelia Sandoval was broken, but not because of her husband's murder—hers were fractures that happened long ago. "I understand." Decklin hesitated, briefly considering leaving the rest of his interview for another time—if there were one.

But, he couldn't.

"Do you consider your husband emotionally or mentally abusive," he asked, fully understanding his question could be his last for the day.

"Both—and, not just to me. Our boys, too . . ."

An interesting reply.

"Thank you for being so candid, Mrs. Sandoval . . . but, one thing keeps coming up in my efforts to find out who murdered Hector—and, perhaps, your husband."

"What's that, Mr. Kilgarry?"

"Santeria—do you know anything about Hector or your husband's being involved?"

Suddenly, Amelia's face set, her jaw tightening. "No—I know nothing about it."

"But, you do know about Santeria, correct?"

"Everyone in my culture knows about it, Mr. Kilgarry, but that doesn't mean everyone practices it."

"Do you?" It was a question Decklin wasn't planning on asking, but, as he spoke the words, he felt her answer was critical to his investigation.

"My religious preferences are none of your business, Mr. Kilgarry, and I fail to see what your question has to do with my husband's murder. Or, Hector's . . ." Amelia stood, then headed for her villa's front door, signaling an end to the interview. "Our conversation is over, Mr. Kilgarry."

Decklin nodded, then followed. "My intent wasn't to offend—please accept my apology."

Amelia focused on him for a few seconds as if she were weighing his words. "I believe you, Mr. Kilgarry—and, if you can shed light on Thomas's murder, I'll be forever in your debt . . ."

So, with that, Decklin Kilgarry left Mrs. Thomas Sandoval to mull things over. If she had anything to do with her husband's murder—or, knew about facts she refused to disclose, time wouldn't be her friend. Murder proves to be a nasty bit of business and, usually, it takes time to unravel the truth. *Was she involved with passing intel,* Decklin wondered as he drove toward his condo. *If that's the case . . .*

But, what Decklin really wanted to know?

Was Colbie Colleen keeping him in the dark?

CHAPTER 18

By the time he arrived home, Decklin had no doubt he and Colbie needed to have a heart-to-heart even though she earlier indicated she'd tell him everything—something Decklin doubted. Though he understood her reluctance to keep him in the loop, he also realized keeping mum had him running in circles. *If she knows Amelia Sandoval is involved with passing intel, it's time I know the truth . . .*

Grabbing a beer from the fridge, he settled on the couch then pulled his cell from his pocket. *No time like the present,* he thought as he tapped Colbie's number on speed dial.

No answer.

Probably a good thing, too, since he wasn't sure what he wanted to say. A few minutes later, however?

A text.

Yes? What's up?

Decklin smiled, fully expecting she'd waste no time getting to the point. *I'll offer the same concise courtesy,* Decklin thought as he typed his response.

Available time?

As he waited for a response, he kicked off his shoes, the conversation with Amelia still on his mind. However, in the middle of questioning everything, his cell chirped.

Tomorrow at 1:00. #3

After a quick confirmation, Decklin tossed his cell on the couch, determined to put Hector's murder on hold for the rest of the evening. *Tomorrow,* he thought as he closed his eyes. *Tomorrow . . .*

The morning nearly gone, Gisele looked up from her work, stunned to see Gloria Fuentes standing in front of her desk—an unfortunate consequence of an unlocked office door. "Did we have an appointment, Gloria? If so, I confess I must not have written it on my calendar . . ."

"No—but, I'm afraid we have business to discuss that can't wait."

Wishing she were anywhere else, Gisele gestured to the small table and chairs in front of her office window. "Please—may I get you something to drink?"

Gloria shook her head, her eyes still on the woman who was really at the helm of Allied International Shipping. "No, thank you—what I have to discuss won't take long."

So, that didn't sound good.

"Then, what can I do for you," Gisele asked, noting Gloria was still standing in front of her desk.

"If you recall our last conversation," Gloria began, her voice offering nothing pleasant, "you assured me our arrangement was possible. Clearly, it's not . . ."

Gisele said nothing for a moment as irritation began to mount. "I have no idea what you're talking about—I've been following the numbers, and Allied International has honored our verbal agreement."

"Then we must agree to disagree . . ." With that, Gloria silently headed for the door. Stepping across the threshold, she suddenly turned, her expression one of determination. "Unfortunately, it will be you who pays the price . . ."

"I finally met with Amelia Sandoval," Decklin began as soon as Colbie sat down. Different than their past meetings, he decided it was he who should be driving the bus if he were to get the answers he needed. "I was asking her questions because Analena rehired me to find out who killed her husband."

"Do you think she had anything to do with it," Colbie asked.

"No—and, I don't think Amelia had anything to do with Thomas's murder. She was, however, somewhat offended when I mentioned Santeria . . ."

Colbie focused on the ocean's waves lapping against the sand as she listened, sensing Decklin was different. "So, what do you need from me?"

Decklin hesitated, knowing what he was about to say could end his working relationship with someone he truly admired. "The truth . . ."

"About what?"

"How Hector, Thomas, and whomever else is passing intel." Decklin paused, trying to get a handle on Colbie's response. "We know they're passing it, but we don't know the order, as well as exactly who's involved—and, I think you do."

"You're right."

Decklin said nothing for a second, surprised by Colbie's being so forthcoming. "I just think . . ."

"No—I don't blame you for asking, and the truth is I should've been up front with you from the beginning." Colbie shifted toward him, then rested her arm on the back of the bench. "The truth is I fought for you to join me on this case because I know you can be an asset—you can get to places I can't, especially since no one recognizes you here except a handful of people."

That was true—when Colbie met Decklin, there was something about him cueing her to the fact he had a talent for pulling information from those who don't feel like talking.

"Why did you have to fight for me?"

"I never got a reason—but, eventually I won, but with the caveat I only divulge certain information."

As Colbie spoke, Decklin couldn't help wondering why she chose to work with the Feds. After all, she had a profitable investigation firm and, to him, it seemed a lot easier. "Now?"

"I need to be honest—but, not here." For the first time in their working relationship, Colbie recognized she wasn't the one to dictate when and where, yet she must. "I'm staying at a hotel on the strip . . ." Suddenly, she rifled through her messenger bag, producing a ripped piece of paper and a pen. Scribbling for a second, she handed it to him. "Here—this is my room number. I'll order in, and we can have a proper conversation . . ."

Without waiting for an answer, she tucked the paper in Decklin's shirt pocket with a smile, stood, then headed along the beach in the opposite direction from which she arrived.

As previously agreed, Decklin held back, choosing to enjoy the briny ocean air for longer than usual. Truth be told, he wasn't comfortable meeting Colbie at her hotel, but it seemed there was little choice. Plucking the paper from his shirt pocket, he unfolded it gently, smiling at its ripped edges.

The Betsy—Rm 305, 6:00 PM

Then, something Decklin didn't expect . . .

I'm sorry . . .

As one might imagine, Gisele Escalante didn't take kindly to threats, so when Gloria Fuentes decided to throw her weight around, the Allied International Shipping exec was having none of it. Allowing Gloria's words to settle before taking action, it wasn't until the following evening did Gisele decide on what she needed to do.

What she must do.

Silently, she stepped onto the part of her veranda that met the watery woods, checking the drawer in the nondescript desk to make certain she had what she needed. Tools for what she had to achieve were many, and it wasn't often she was required to use them. That evening, however?

Prudent to have them at hand.

Gently, she removed her sandals, then took her seat on the small stool as she prepared herself for casting a spell—something not regularly used within the Santeria religion. *Just this once*, she promised herself, though she knew her thought was a lie. The truth was Gisele Escalante had no compunction about doing anything required to realize a successful ritual.

A sliver of a smile on her lips as she collected what she needed, Gisele quietly chanted to herself as she constructed a doll crafted from muslin, then drew Santeria symbols on it to seal her wishes. Her desires. And, it was then she decided to use her Macumba skills, casting a spell of irreversible damage to its recipient, knowing she must wait patiently for its effects.

"When the time is right," she chanted, "so shall it be. So shall it be . . ."

CHAPTER 19

As Decklin stood in front of Colbie's hotel room door, there was no denying he felt a little weird. Though he understood her predilection for maintaining privacy, perhaps such a meeting was going a little too far. *Too late now,* he thought as he raised his hand to knock. Just then, the door opened, Colbie grinning like a little kid as she greeted him. "I knew you were here," she confessed, stepping to the side allowing Decklin to enter.

"Of course, you did . . ."

"I took the liberty of ordering a bite to eat—I always think better on a full stomach. I hope you don't mind . . ."

"I don't—in fact, that sounds good since I haven't eaten all day."

"All day? Not good . . ."

"I know, but I guess I typify everything you hear about the life of a bachelor . . ."

"Well, perhaps that's a conversation for another day. For now, throw your jacket wherever and let's get to work!"

As Decklin made himself comfortable, he scanned the room as Colbie rounded up appetizers delivered prior to his arrival. Files were strewn on a table large enough to seat six comfortably, offering plenty of room to stretch out. "Nice digs!"

"Thanks—a bit much for my taste, but I take what they give me." From that point forward?

All work.

"First," Colbie offered as she plucked grapes, bleu cheese and crackers from a hand carved charcuterie board, "I'd like to officially apologize for being an idiot . . ."

"An idiot? I don't think that's—"

"Necessary? Yes, it is—for some reason, while working this case, I find myself boxed in by people who really know nothing about me other than what I do for a living." A brief pause for a bite. "And, as I continue—I've been embedded for over a year—I realize I'm compromising myself."

"In what way," Decklin asked, joining her with a bite of his own.

"Only that I don't feel as if I'm in control—someone else is always pulling the strings."

"But, isn't that always the way when working for clients? I mean, they have the purse strings, so they usually want things done their way." Another bite. "Really, there are only a few who allow us the leeway to do what we do best—and, money talks."

Colbie leaned back in her chair, patting her lips with a linen napkin. "I knew you'd get it—but, right now, my need for autonomy isn't the issue. I have a story to tell . . ."

"I'm all ears . . ."

A quick drink of water. "I know you've been waffling about what Analena and Amelia have to do, if anything, with their husbands' deaths—and, the answer is nothing. Both were in difficult marriages, but for different reasons. Sadly, Hector didn't recognize what he had at home . . ."

"What about Sandoval?"

"Even worse, I suppose, Thomas didn't care what he had at home—money was his prime motivator, similar to Hector, but Thomas took his need to a different level. He didn't care what he had to do to make himself feel worthy, and verbally abusing his wife was part of the package when it came to social fame."

"If that's the case, why did the Feds approach him to embed?"

"Because he would do anything to make himself feel socially elevated. He needed admiration in his life, so when the Feds came calling, he was more than willing to answer."

"Not sure I understand . . ."

"It's simple, really—even though he had more than enough money, in his mind it just wasn't so."

"So, I'm guessing your higher-ups offered a nice chunk of change to tell them everything he learned about Hector, and whomever else is involved with their case."

"Exactly."

"What about Amelia? If he were such an ass, why did she stay with him? I imagine if they split, she'd be taken care of for the rest of her life."

"One would think—but, who's to say what goes on behind closed doors. The only thing interesting me about Amelia is her connection to Santeria—and, Macumba."

"Macumba? What the hell is that?"

"A black magic ritual—a powerful one."

Decklin swallowed hard, uncertain if he wanted to hear what Colbie had to say. The whole Santeria thing had him spooked more than he wanted to admit, and he was sure Colbie knew. "Okay . . ."

"Few things are off the table in both spiritual practices, but Macumba, in my opinion, is darker. Harsher. It's origin is Africa merged with Brazil—and, interestingly, Macumba isn't an actual religion. It's a form of Vodun and Santeria, worshipping ancient African gods by means of spirit possession." Glancing at Decklin, Colbie reached for more grapes. "There's more, but that's really all you need to know—unless you want to know gory details."

"No thanks—I'll take your suggestion, and leave it there. I'm not too hip on possession . . ."

A smile. "I thought so . . ."

"What I'm wondering," Decklin replied, "is whether Macumba is practiced by a regular person, or is it reserved for those who were born into or studied it."

A quick sip of water. "Excellent question, Detective Kilgarry! It's both, I suppose—but, I think there's a predilection toward the former."

"Interesting—so, is Macumba Amelia's main thing?"

"Another good question, and the answer is I don't really know. I know, though someone who knows a lot about it . . ."

An impish grin. "Care to share?"

Colbie laughed, shooting him a good-natured dagger. "Say that again, and we're done!"

Smiling, Decklin plucked a few crackers and two slices of cheese from the charcuterie board. "Objection noted—so, who's the Macumba master?"

"Gisele Escalante."

Decklin stared at Colbie for a moment, his thoughts taking a dark turn. "Wait—she's your contact."

"Yep—but, I'm pretty sure she's not on our side."

That was news.

For months, Colbie entertained thoughts of Gisele's being involved in their case, but in a different manner than originally thought. Of course, she didn't have proof, so it remained a possibility rather than a certainty.

So, she kept her mouth shut.

"When we got wind of the Santeria ritual—the one you witnessed—I went to the ceremony to tune in to see if Gisele were someone other than the practitioner she let others see."

"Is she?"

"The jury's still out . . ."

Devon watched as Analena Cortina departed the Catholic church with a little too much pep in her step, something he found odd for someone who was planning a funeral—at least, that's what he suspected she was doing. *A signal Hector's body is about to be released,* he wondered as he kept binos trained on her. *And, why the hell are you making funeral arrangements in the evening?*

For a moment, he considered popping into the church to get the lay of the land, knowing Decklin and Colbie would probably attend the funeral surreptitiously. But, even though knowing nooks and crannies could be helpful, Devon didn't feel comfortable snooping around when someone working for the church was there—and, he didn't feel like losing Analena to do so.

Watching as she pulled her classy sports car away from the curb, he couldn't help noticing her shit-eatin' grin. *Me thinks you're ready to be done with Hector,* Devon thought. *So, let's see where you go . . .*

What Devon didn't see?

The tail he picked up as soon as he left the office.

"What I haven't mentioned to anyone," Colbie continued, "is I've been having intuitive impressions about an explosion—but, I'm not sure if it symbolizes an actual explosion or pent up anger."

As much as Decklin wanted to ask her about how visions and impressions came to her, he figured it would be an invasion of privacy. "So, you'd like to know how it all works," she suddenly asked, the childish grin returning.

"Well . . ."

"Here's the truth—I'm no different than anyone else. Anyone—you included—can do the same thing."

"Oh, c'mon!"

"It's true! All of us have the same abilities, but so many refuse to use them. Which, by the way, I find incredibly interesting since every damned one of us has commented on 'gut feelings.'"

Decklin placed his napkin on the table, then sat back in his seat, hunger satiated. "That was really good—thank you!"

Colbie smiled, pushed her chair back, then settled into a comfortable position. "You also want to know how things come to me . . ."

Decklin blushed, slightly unnerved.

"Sometimes, it's like watching a movie—other times, I receive information in symbols. Like the explosion . . . I saw The Tower card in a tarot deck. It's a card of destruction, sudden change, and chaos."

"Great—yours or someone else's?" Of course, Decklin had never seen a tarot card in his life, and he wasn't about to start.

"Someone else." A brief pause to continue her thread concerning their case. "So, back to Gisele Escalante—for now, it's enough to know my radar is in full gear, and it's time we treat her as someone other than an informant."

"Meaning?"

"If you're amenable, stick to her as much as you can. I want to see who she meets and where she goes."

"Including where she works? At Allied International Shipping?"

"Especially there—and, take snacks. Chances are good it's going to be a boring gig, but it has to be done." Colbie paused, hoping Decklin was on board. "What do you think?"

That was interesting! Asking Decklin what he truly thought laid to rest any doubt he had about her. Even so, he wasn't thrilled with the idea. "Devon and I can switch on and off—I'm getting too old to be crammed into a car all day!"

So, with that settled, Decklin took his leave, promising Colbie he'd be in touch soon. As they parted at her hotel room door, she suddenly took his hand, giving it a squeeze, then tucked a piece of paper in his jacket pocket. "Again, I'm sorry—I should've been honest from the beginning."

A quick squeeze in return.

Nothing said.

As South Beach turned rowdy and wrapped in evening heat, Gisele Escalante returned her ritual items to their desk drawer, making certain each was placed in a particular position. Then, an unfamiliar sound. "Who's there," she called, then waited for a response.

Nothing.

Yet, she was sure—she knew. Standing at the edge of her veranda, she scanned the murky water, certain something or someone was lurking. "I know you're there!"

Suddenly, the muffled sound of running feet.

Gisele stood still, sending out intuitive feelers toward the unwelcome visitor, but she felt little. *Perhaps, I'm mistaken*, she thought, though she knew better.

With nothing more, she extinguished the candles, then stood silently again, listening. Finally, as she turned to leave her altar for the evening, it was then she noticed—a coral snake, its poison capable of dropping anyone to their knees, slithering in front of her door as if waiting to perform its deadly duty. It's calling.

Unafraid, Gisele stepped away, allowing plenty of room, convinced it would be gone by morning. A coincidence?

Probably not.

A final time, she peered into the darkness, the hair on her arms standing at attention. *Whoever you are, she promised, you will be mine . . .*

A silent threat?

Indeed.

By the time Decklin returned to his condo, it was still early, especially according to South Beach standards. Unwilling to let opportunity pass, he fished for the small piece of paper Colbie slipped into his jacket pocket as he left her hotel room, knowing it was Gisele Escalante's address.

Only taking time to change into his black linen summer shirt, he grabbed a bottle of water, then headed out the door, hoping to reach his destination within thirty. Without knowing the area well, however, finding it could take awhile.

By ten o'clock, South Beach was in full swing with partying, blaring music, and revelers spilling into the streets with little consideration for cars and, as much as Decklin wanted to ignore them, doing so was impossible. Counting the minutes until he arrived in Gisele's part of town, it was a welcome relief when he arrived at a place perfect for the Santeria high priestess, yet a disconnect when considering her job. Her career. Tucked against the black water's edge, her cabin was modest with soft lamplight illuminating only one room. *This is how an executive for Allied International lives*, he asked himself as he drove by. *Creepy . . .*

Parking far enough away to not arouse suspicion, Decklin settled in for the long haul as he cut the engine, then reached for a Twix bar in the center console. Placing it next to his binos, he sat back, scanned the area, then cycled through his earlier conversation with Colbie—until he noticed someone approaching Gisele's home, a small crate in hand.

What the hell? Grabbing the binos, Decklin watched, fully aware the person knew where he—or, she—was going, disappearing to the back of the house. Emerging minutes later with the crate, the intruder glanced left and right, then vanished into the darkness.

What the hell was that all about, Decklin wondered as he returned his focus to Gisele's home. Whatever it was?

He knew it wasn't good.

CHAPTER 20

*I*t was only by luck that Devon Bryson happened to notice Analena Cortina walking out of a posh, designer store on South Beach with a woman who could've stopped traffic. Tall, lanky, and statuesque, the two women obviously had a couple of things in common—expensive taste, and the money to fulfill unbridled fashion desires. Though he didn't recognize Analena's friend, he couldn't help thinking there was something familiar about her. Though, to be accurate, there were a lot of striking women in Miami, and she really blended in with the crowd—the only thing catching his attention was the fact she was with Analena.

They're obviously friends, Devon considered as he watched them disappear into another designer store, one of several open in the evening to accommodate tourists. Mere feet from the one they just left, it was clear the women knew each other well. *Or, sisters . . .* A good thought, too, as he focused on the shop's front door—both had long black hair, accentuated by perfect features and ageless skin. A clue Hector worked on both to achieve desired perfection?

Probably.

So, with that thought, Devon inched past the store's entrance, making note of the time and place. *Maybe it's something,* he mused as he watched the car in front of him try to gain leverage in the snarled traffic. *Or, nothing . . .*

With little to show for his efforts, Decklin called it a night, realizing Gisele was, most likely, in for the evening. Even so, leaving a surveillance with nothing to show for it wasn't Decklin Kilgarry's style and, knowing he could pick up his surveillance the following day, offered only tepid consolation. He did have one thing, however . . .

The person with the crate.

It would be easy for someone with a slight, wiry build to slip through the shadows without detection, and Decklin knew that's exactly what the person was trying to do. *Male or female,* he wondered as he eased into South Beach traffic after stopping for a late-night coffee. *Hard to tell—either way, the whole thing's just plain weird. And, with Gisele's Santeria expertise, who the hell knows what's going on?*

But, as much as he didn't want to look into it further, Decklin knew he must—besides, it was better than putting Devon onto something that scared the livin' crap out of him. So, when Devon messaged his partner about seeing Analena with a friend that evening, it was a welcome diversion—at least for an hour or two.

"Any idea of who it was," Decklin asked when they connected the following day.

"Nope—but, I'm wondering if she's related to Analena. They kind of looked alike—you know, perfect."

"Then, that makes me wonder if the other woman was also Hector's patient . . ."

"Same here—but, I'm guessing we'll never know. Probably nothing more than a friend or relative . . ."

As much as Decklin wanted to learn more, there were other things on their docket. "Don't forget we have to mingle at the Cuban festival this weekend . . ." he advised, underscoring it's importance. "I figure it's a solid bet Carmen Santosa will be there, and I don't want to miss a chance to lay eyes on her . . ."

"Agreed—so, are we switching?"

"You mean is it your turn to surveil Gisele?" Decklin didn't wait for an answer, more than happy to turn his duties over to his young partner. "Yes . . ." And, as much as he wanted to, he decided against clueing Devon in on the person with the small crate. With how he felt about Santeria?

He didn't really need to know.

In the private investigator biz, nothing yields more information than attending the funeral of a murder victim, instilling investigators with good ideas regarding the deceased's friends and colleagues. Unfortunately, Thomas Sandoval's send-off didn't amount to much even though there was a full-sized casket, leaving Decklin to hope Hector's final goodbye would be more profitable. But, as Decklin, Devon, and Colbie filed into the church to pay their respects to Hector, each noticed a disappointing suspect pool. "Shouldn't there be a lot more people here," Devon whispered to Decklin before taking their individual seats apart from each other.

A nod. "One would think—and, the fact there are so few makes me wonder about things we haven't considered."

Colbie said nothing as she sidled into the second pew to stake her presence next to Aidan Lopez. Prior to their arrival, she decided to be up front while Decklin and Devon assumed positions at the rear of the church as well as the side. Each had a good view of Hector's casket and mourners, none of whom seemed to be too interested as the priest took his place in front of them. *Only here out of obligation*, Devon recognized as he caught Decklin's eye and slight nod of approval for Devon's position in the church.

And, his thought certainly appeared to be the truth—an hour later, those attending filed out the door, most picking up their pace as they headed to their cars after filing through the reception line. "So, did you notice anything," Devon asked when he met up with Decklin and Colbie.

"Nothing," Decklin advised, "and, it's odd there weren't more people attending, which makes me wonder who didn't have much use for Hector."

"As I sat next to Aidan, I tuned in on him, and he could care less about Hector's murder. In fact, he was hoping he wasn't next on the list—something I found quite intriguing." As Colbie spoke, she kept an eye on mourners filing from the church, her gut telling her someone involved in Hector's murder was close.

Decklin said little as they made their way to their respective vehicles until he spied a familiar face walking away from them. "It appears Gisele Escalante was here . . . "

"Seriously? I didn't see her . . ." Colbie glanced at Devon, noting his surprise, as well.

"Nor did I—which tells me she either slipped in after we were seated, or she chose a spot a bit more secluded."

"That tells us a lot, don't you think?" Devon stopped as they reached the parking lot. "If she were mourning Hector's passing, why wouldn't she sit with the rest of them?"

As he was speaking, Decklin recalled the recent conversation at Colbie's hotel when they discussed Gisele's possible involvement in their case. "There's only one reason I can think of," he finally commented as he fished his keys out of his jacket pocket.

Colbie nodded, glancing at Anderson who was waiting for her a few spaces from Decklin's car. "Obviously, she didn't want anyone to know she was here . . ."

By the time Saturday rolled around, a driving, vicious rain claimed Miami, canceling the Cuban Festival while destroying the possibility of getting eyes on Carmen Santosa within her own habitat. "So, now what," Devon asked when he met Decklin for breakfast. "I can tail her, if you want . . ."

By his tone, Decklin recognized his partner was getting a bit bored with his detail of following Analena—something he was tasked with since the beginning of their investigation. "Good idea—it's time we turn our attention to the main players." And, that was true, especially since Decklin learned Analena and Amelia weren't responsible for their husbands' respective murders—or, anything else. Clearly, it was time to turn their attention elsewhere. "Begin at the U.S. Embassy, and tail her from the time she arrives at work."

"I'll get there early to get a view of the parking lot," Devon agreed.

"Excellent—don't let her out of your sight, and I want to know everything, especially if she visits the Cuban Consulate or goes anywhere near there."

"Got it—but, today's a washout."

"Agreed—take the weekend to enjoy yourself, and start on Monday." Decklin smiled, knowing Devon would relish a couple of days off in a row. "You've earned it . . ."

With a smile, Devon saluted as he headed toward his car, neither man aware of the black sedan parked directly across the street. A misstep?

Yes.

As much as Decklin wanted to spend a rainy Saturday night in front of his television and snagging a good night's sleep, it wasn't meant to be. Just as he settled in for a comfy night, his cell chirped. "This better be good," he chided when he picked up, knowing it was Devon. "What's up?"

"I picked up a tail . . ."

Instantly, Decklin sat up, grabbing his notepad and pen. "Vehicle?"

"Black Cadillac sedan—new, '23 or '24."

"Driver?"

"Can't see because of the rain—but, he's been on me since I left my place. Obviously, whoever it is, knows where I live . . ."

Exactly what Decklin didn't want to hear. "Where are you now?"

"Driving south on the A1A—I'm on my way to meet my date."

Decklin thought for a moment, knowing Devon could be putting someone else in danger if he didn't lose the tail. "Abort. Message your date to let her know there's an emergency—you can't take the chance of putting her in an unsafe situation."

Recognizing Decklin's serious tone, Devon agreed. "Done. I'll head home . . ."

"Keep me posted, and let me know when you reach your place." But, before Devon could confirm, the call dropped, leaving Decklin to wonder if it were due to weather or something else. After a couple of hours, however, and with no word from his partner, he began to worry, knowing he needed to make Colbie aware of the situation. *Maybe she can tune into him,* he thought, recognizing there was a time he wouldn't have considered such a thing as he tapped her number on speed dial. "Will you please tune into Devon," he asked before explaining. "He may be in trouble . . ."

"Don't tell me anything," she instantly replied. "It'll be easier for me—and, I'm picking up he's in his car."

"Correct."

Then, what her colleague didn't want to hear. "He's in trouble, Deck . . ."

Decklin waited, hoping she could pick up on more, but that was it. "I'll let you know if I see anything else," she finally commented. "Please keep me in the loop . . ."

Assuring he would do so, Decklin sat back on his couch as his cell screen faded, figuring out logistics. Never having been to Devon's apartment, it made more sense to stay put and wait for him to get in touch.

So, there he sat, cell in hand as he waited for his partner's call—one that never came. One that did, however?

Florida Mercy Hospital.

When Decklin confirmed he was Devon's emergency contact, a nurse explained the reason for her call. "Devon is in the emergency room—he was severely beaten, and he asked us to notify you."

Out the door.

Flirting with a reason to get a traffic ticket on the way to the hospital, Decklin texted Colbie . . .

911—Miami Mercy

Within twenty, he pulled on the emergency entrance door and headed for the reception desk, scanning everyone in the waiting room. Waiting for the receptionist to get off the phone, she finally looked up at him, her blue eyes intense, yet caring. "How can I help you?"

"I'm here about Devon Bryson," Decklin explained, knowing he probably couldn't see Devon until after he were treated.

A quick tap on her computer keyboard. "Oh, yes—Mr. Bryson's waiting for a doctor to see him to determine the extent of his injuries."

Decklin's heart dropped, fully understanding the enormity of the situation. "May I see him?"

Glancing at the waiting room filled with patients, the receptionist hesitated, then made a decision. "He's in number nine," she advised, motioning to the doors leading to the circular corridor of treatment rooms. "I'll let you in."

Thanking her, Decklin waited for the doors to open, trying not to glance in each room as he hurried down the hallway. Quickly locating Devon's room, he opened the door quietly, his stomach lurching at what he saw, the taste of vomit rising into his mouth. Lying on his back, Devon's head lolled to the left, exposing the right side of his lacerated face, his right eye swollen shut, his jaw in similar condition.

Not surprised by the extensive injuries, Decklin silently pulled up a chair to Devon's bedside, sitting for a full twenty minutes, watching his young friend as he slept. Noticing a pad and paper on a small, metal table, Decklin realized Devon might not be able to speak due to his jaw injury.

Waking moments later, though he was groggy and in pain, Devon scanned the room, noticing the pad and pen. Catching Devon's glance, Decklin handed them to him, waiting as his partner wrote slowly, then showed the pad to his partner.

"The hospital called—where else would I be?"

Then, what Decklin needed to know as Devon struggled to write again. "The tail . . ."

As much as Decklin wanted to hear exactly what happened, it was clear Devon was in no shape to provide information. "I know," Decklin replied, "but, now's not the time. I'll be here for as long as I can," Decklin promised as the emergency room doctor showed up. "Should I notify your parents?"

A slight nod.

Minutes later, Decklin watched as a nurse joined the physician, the doctor wasting no time as he began questioning his patient. *Whoever did this,* Decklin silently promised as Devon tried to speak, *will pay . . .*

Closing the door gently, Decklin made his way back to the emergency waiting room, taking a seat moments before Colbie arrived, cell in hand. "I was just going to text you to let you know I'm here," she commented as she sat beside him. "What do you know?"

"You probably already know—but, it's not good. Someone beat the livin' shit out of Devon, leaving him with a bashed in face and an injured jaw."

"Holy shit! Did they let you see him?"

"Yes, but it was brief—not long after I got to see him, a nurse showed up. Besides, it was hard for him to talk, so I didn't want to push it . . ."

Digesting what Decklin told her, Colbie fully understood the implications. "The stench of cartel," she finally responded, knowing damned well Devon's getting the shit kicked out of him was a clear message.

"I figured—but, we really won't know anything until later. So . . ."

Grasping Decklin's hand, she gave it a reassuring squeeze. "I'm staying . . ."

Gloria Fuentes sat behind her father's desk, glaring at her best operative. "Misión cumplida," he advised, a grin crossing his lips as he recalled beating Devon Bryson.

"¿Está vivo?"

A nod. "Como ordenaste . . ."

"Yes—as I ordered." With that, Gloria waved her hand in dismissal, waiting until her best man left, leaving her to relish the thrill of success. Though slightly built, Manuel always struck like a coiled rattler, making the best of unsuspecting prey. *No one,* she thought as she lit a cigarette, *sticks their nose into my business without paying the price . . .*

Was such action something her father would've done? Probably not—but, in her mind, he was spending time in a pricey mausoleum, and what he would've thought or done simply didn't matter. Hers was a position to savor, the spark of power spreading to every molecule of her body as she enjoyed her expected rewards. Should someone notice her pleasure, one would think it wasn't her first time issuing such an order. Of course, that wasn't the case, but it did take guts, and that was enough for the new cartel boss.

Proving she was a force within her pivoting organization, her message wasn't only delivered to Devon Bryson, it targeted anyone denying her rightful place as her father's daughter. *Now,* she thought, smiling, *on to the next . . .*

CHAPTER 21

"Remember when I told you about my vision of The Tower— the tarot card advising of destruction and chaos," Colbie asked as she and Decklin waited for news regarding the extent of Devon's injuries.

"Of course—what about it?"

"This is it."

Understandably, Decklin didn't quite know what to say—he knew nothing about such things and any question he had would probably sound ridiculous. So, instead, he opted for the obvious. "What's next," he asked, knowing it would be a cold day before he'd give up on finding the person responsible for Devon's beating. "He was taken to the mat, Colbie . . ."

"I understand—and, I already alerted Anderson and my team. This won't be taken lightly . . ."

"Who do you think put out the hit?"

Colbie paused, then looked Decklin dead in the eye. "Gloria Fuentes—there's no doubt in my mind. She meant to deliver a message, meaning we're now on her radar."

As Decklin was about to respond, the receptionist motioned to him. "Devon was moved," she explained, her tone cool and clinical. "Room 103 . . ."

Thanking her, Decklin motioned for Colbie to join him. "He's in a room," he explained as they followed signs to the elevators. "That didn't take as long as I expected . . ."

"What a relief!"

Waiting for an elevator that wasn't crammed with hospital visitors, five minutes passed before Decklin knocked gently on Devon's door. "Dev?"

With tubes connected to his arm, Devon motioned them in. "I'm sorry . . ." At least, that's what Decklin thought he said—Devon's words were mush.

"Sorry? For what, for God's sake?" As he spoke, Decklin felt a resurging anger.

Devon tried licking his lips, then motioned to a cup of water on the bedside stand.

Interpreting quickly, Colbie handed it to him. "Slowly— drink slowly," she advised, making sure the straw was tilted. Once Devon took a sip, he tried to smile, then pointed to a tablet and pen. "Good idea," Colbie replied, smiling as she handed them to him.

"Only if you feel like it," Decklin advised as he plucked his notepad from his jacket pocket. "If not, we'll wait . . ." Silence. "Take your time . . ."

Again, Devon licked his lips, then began writing . . .

Gas station—2

"There were two of them," Colbie asked.

A nod and more writing . . .

Dragged me to side kicked

"I'm guessing they pulled you over to the side so they wouldn't be within camera view," Colbie commented.

"Good point—did you get a look at either one of them," Decklin asked, hoping for the answer he needed.

Devon shook his head.

Cadillac

As much as Decklin wanted to ask more questions, he knew doing so was too much. Ordering Devon to get some rest, he and Colbie quietly left his room, Decklin noticing Devon was already dozing off as he closed the door gently. Standing in the corridor for a moment, he scanned the hallway, aware of patients needing care, and he could only imagine how difficult hospitals must be for Colbie.

"Let's get the hell out of here," she suddenly suggested as they headed toward the elevators. "Dinner or breakfast?"

A nod. "Your place or mine?"

Carmen Santos stared at her reflection in the mirror as she did every morning and evening, then stripped off her wig, tossing it on the bathroom counter. As if analyzing something important, she peered closely at her face, fully understanding gravity continued to show its effect—a realization giving rise to an unanticipated blood pressure spike. In her mind?

Hector Cortina was to blame.

Of course, after Hector was murdered, one might think her reason for just revenge was quashed, but it simply wasn't so. The way Carmen saw it, there were plenty of lives she could make miserable, and that's exactly what she intended to do. If she couldn't make Hector pay, his family would do just as well—though, to be fair, she did have a slight reservation when it came to ruining his children's lives.

A thought quickly banished.

Luckily, due to Hector's ineptitude, Carmen knew how to mask her deficiencies and imperfections with makeup, so, when she inserted herself into Analena's life after her husband's passing, there was no recognition. It really wasn't surprising, though, since she only met Carmen Santosa once or twice. With a few alterations and an expensive black wig?

Maria Valdez was born.

None the wiser, Analena graciously accepted her new friend into her private circle, giving no thought to the possibility her life was about to change. Far-fetched? Of course. But, the truth was Analena really wasn't too bright—

at least, that's what Hector thought. To him, she was little more than a pretty bauble for his arm—and, he felt that way for a considerable time.

Chuckling, Carmen snatched the wig from the counter, placing it on its stand, then headed for a small wet bar in her den. Pouring a stiff shot of whiskey, she winced as it warmed her throat, reminding her of her father's evening ritual. But, as much as Carmen would've loved to dive into familial memories, she had other things on her mind— Gloria Fuentes for one.

You're overplaying your hand, Carmen thought as she knocked back a another shot before preparing for a scheduled drop—and, when thinking about it, she was right. It was obvious Gloria was flexing her muscles, something that could, potentially, interfere with Carmen's lifestyle. Always doing her best to fly under the radar, as far as she knew, no one had a clue of her treasonous duplicity, and that's the way she wanted to keep it. But, with Gloria's making her presence known?

The Feds would notice.

The only problem was there was no proof to confirm Carmen's suspicions of cartel involvement with her own mission of doing what was right for her home country. Knowing the Miami mafia pledged no allegiance to the Cuban regime, the only reason for their possible involvement was money—something Carmen found reprehensible, even though she was being paid by them for passing intel. Even so, she was well aware that's all she did, and nothing else was involved.

Still, though little more than a pawn in a dangerous game, it made Carmen Santosa feel like a million bucks, and it was then she decided to take matters into her own hands. With her contact pool dwindling due to Thomas's and

Hector's untimely demise, it was up to her to find someone
she could trust. Someone who wouldn't ask questions.
Someone who was more interested in the finer things in life
than what really matters—such as loyalty to one's culture.
One's country.

Someone like Analena Cortina.

"I contacted Devon's parents, and they're on the next
flight from Boston," Decklin informed Colbie as he rifled
through the refrigerator for something he could turn into
a finished meal. "Do you like pork chops," he asked as
Colbie watched various items make their way to the kitchen
counter. Suddenly, Decklin emerged from the fridge. "Did
you eat already?"

Laughing, Colbie pulled out a chair at the island. "No,
but I think pork chops might be a little heavy . . ."

"That's all I have . . ."

"How about if I order something for delivery? That
way you don't have to cook . . ." Colbie rifled through her
messenger bag for her phone, then tapped the screen.
"What's your fancy?"

"You choose—as long as I don't have to cook it, I'm
good!"

So, minutes later and with snack decisions made, Decklin and Colbie made their way to the living room, glasses of wine in hand. "Make yourself comfortable," Decklin invited, gesturing to the couch. "It's been a long night—feel free to kick your shoes off." Leading by example, he slipped off his loafers, then joined her as she made herself comfortable. "Cheers . . ."

Following his lead, Colbie tucked her legs beneath her, turning toward him. "I don't mind saying this whole thing with Devon is really pissing me off . . ."

"Me, too—and, I'm sure as hell not going to stop looking for whoever did it." Decklin shifted slightly so he could focus on her, draping his arm across the back of the couch. "So, tell me why you think it's Gloria Fuentes . . ."

"Because she has the most to gain—and, it's time we look at the end game. She's the ruler of Miami's strongest, most vicious cartel—and, she has something to prove. We recently uncovered chatter among her own about a coup— seems a few of her own aren't too thrilled with the new regime."

Decklin said nothing, knowing Colbie would continue.

"And, there's no doubt Gloria knows about the unrest, and that's not a good thing . . ." Colbie paused, thinking of how things were playing out. "Like I said, she has something to prove—so, when she learned of our involvement, rearranging Devon's face was a good way to make a statement."

"The question is," Decklin replied, "how did she find out about us?"

Again, Colbie was quiet for a few seconds. "You're right— that's the question. We suspect the cartel is in bed with Aidan Lopez's shipping company, but getting confirmation has been painfully slow." A pause. "Gisele Escalante is part of the equation, and we suspect . . ."

"You don't know?"

"No—I'm certain of it, but my handlers want to be rock-solid sure before making a move."

Decklin sipped his wine, saying nothing for a few moments, until he knew he needed to ask the question that was on his mind for weeks. "How do you do it," he asked, knowing she may not answer. "It seems to me you're being held back because of the government's inability to make a decision that will protect our country . . ."

"I admit, it's been difficult . . ."

"Well, can't you quit and proceed on your own?"

"I could, I suppose—I wouldn't be sanctioned, of course."

Sensing something Colbie didn't want to share, Decklin decided it was time to be truthful with her. "I'm the first one to admit I have no knowledge regarding governmental treason—I was only a D.C. detective. But, the whole thing makes me wonder if your investigation—and, mine—is being slow-walked."

"I have to admit, I have the same concerns—and, it makes me feel as if I'm not only wasting my time, I'm a pawn in a much bigger game."

As much as Decklin wanted to continue their heart-to-heart, a text announcing the arrival of their after-midnight snack interrupted their conversation. Grinning, Decklin rose, then headed to the door. "Hold that thought . . ."

Moments later, he placed the delivery bag on the table, then crossed to the kitchen for plates, utensils, and napkins. "Feel free to spread everything out on the coffee table," he called over his shoulder.

So, within five, both were diving into appetizers, each choosing to top off their glasses of wine. "I have to be honest," Decklin confessed as he finally sat back, hunger satisfied. "I find you curious . . ."

Smiling, Colbie followed suit as she placed her small plate on the coffee table. "In what way?"

"Well, I'm curious if you have a dog in the fight . . ."

"Other than being brought in on a contract gig?"

Decklin was quiet for a moment, wondering if his next words would overstep. "Yes—but, honestly, I can't figure out what that would be."

"Probably because I have no reason to be here other than trying to do the best for my country." Colbie hesitated, knowing her truth may be tough to swallow. "I will say, however, I was becoming bored always being by myself— as much as I traveled around the globe, the luster began to wear off."

"Tarnishing the type of work you were doing?"

A nod. "In a way—I've always been hired for my intuitive abilities in one way or another. But, after studying in Edinburgh, I realized I was embroiled in something I could do, but it didn't bring as much pleasure as when I worked cases involving things outside of my abilities."

"In other words, you were feeling trapped?"

"A little, yes—but, 'unfulfilled' may be more accurate." A sip. "When I first entered the private investigation field, I thought I wanted to be a profiler for the FBI. My path at the time, however, didn't lead me in that direction."

As Decklin listened, he couldn't help wondering if Colbie's losing her long-time partner was the reason for choosing a different avenue. "Where did it lead you?"

"Well, as you know, I did my own thing . . . until life got in the way."

"Meaning?"

Focusing on the wine glass in her hand, Colbie teared up at the memory. "I lost Brian. But, of course, you already knew that . . ."

A flush crept up Decklin's neck as he listened. "You're right—I admit I learned everything I could about you when you entered my life."

A gentle smile. "I hope it was worth reading . . ."

Suddenly, Decklin placed his glass on the coffee table, then pulled her to him, tucking her safely into the crook of his arm. "It was . . ."

And, there they sat, saying nothing, yet feeling everything as sorbet colors of pink and orange graced the horizon. For both?

It had been a long time.

CHAPTER 22

Devon grimaced as Decklin closed the hospital room door, noticing his partner carried a to-go bag loaded with his favorite food. "Hope your jaw is feeling better," he teased as he spread everything on the small table by the bed.

"It is—my arm, however, is another story!"

"What does the doc say?"

"A few weeks with this thing," Devon replied, showing off his sling, "but, I hope to be ready to go after two." Devon paused, eyeing the feast beside him. "I can't lift anything, for a while, though . . ."

"Well, try lifting this lobster roll—it's what the doctor ordered," Decklin suggested. "Eat what you can while I fill you in on details . . ."

So, while Devon picked at the lobster only, Decklin brought his partner up to speed, detailing most of his conversation with Colbie, as well as her thoughts on their case. "It sounds to me," Devon offered, "she's not happy with how things are going. And, to be honest, I have to agree with you and her—progress is too slow." He hesitated, realizing eating was out of the question. "I mean, the Feds have known about this stuff for more than a few years, and I can't wrap my head around why it's taking so long . . ."

As Decklin listened, nagging futility resurfaced, making him wonder if they should bow out of the investigation, allowing Colbie to proceed on her own. "I still come back to the fact we got into this because of Analena's wanting to know if her husband were cheating on her . . ."

"Which," Devon reminded him, "we didn't find out until later."

"True—I guess I'm questioning whether we should be involved, at all. It sure as hell isn't making us any money . . ."

"I know—I'm not worried about money, but it would be nice to be paid for what we're doing."

And, that was the thing—certainly, Colbie was making a nice chunk of change for her part, but no one offered compensation for their being involved in the investigation. "Maybe it's something we need to bring up to Colbie," Devon suggested.

So, by the time Devon ate all he could, he and Decklin decided on one thing. "I don't feel right about ditching Colbie," Decklin finally admitted, wondering if his decision were work related or personal. "So, if you agree, I think we should stick it out . . ."

"I'm in—but, I also think we need to give Colbie a time frame. If nothing's moving forward within the next few weeks, I say we jump ship. I'm not on board for being tied up for months—or, years."

A nod. "I'll let her know . . ."

For the third time, Gisele Escalante sat on her veranda, dissatisfaction brewing in her soul. Focusing on the dark water's edge, an uncontrollable shift coursed through her, one she didn't like one bit. Yet, understanding it was representative of a negative energy preempting her carefully executed plan, there was little she could do except take matters into her own hands.

A position she relished when necessary.

So, as she had done so many times, Gisele extracted ritual tools from the small desk, then opened the manila envelope, revealing a photo of the one person who could take her down. *But,* she realized, *a mere spell isn't enough . . .*

Carefully, she pulled small squares of cream-colored cloth, string, and pins from the drawer, laying each on the tabletop illuminated by nine flickering candles. "It is time," she murmured, her sinewy fingers stroking the cloth as she decided upon her words.

Then, nimbly, she began to work.

Assembling everything she needed, the Santeria High Priestess outlined the shape of a voodoo doll onto two pieces of the fabric, then cut them out, saving the unused portion of cloth for a later ceremony. Next, using embroidery floss, she sewed a button for the right eye and stitched an 'x' for the left, completing the face with a horizontally stitched line for the mouth.

Uttering unintelligible words as she worked, Gisele cut out a small heart from red felt, then stitched it to the doll's chest in the place where a human heart would be. Finally, partially sewing the two pieces of cloth together, she plucked petals from a fresh red rose, stuffing them into the doll, stitching it closed as her final preparation.

Holding the voodoo doll in front of her, she spoke the ritual words to work for eleven days, imbuing it with a darkness created only for revenge.

One present in her soul.

If Decklin learned anything about Colbie in the time they'd been working together, it was her propensity for never giving up. In fact, he told her so when she agreed with his suggestion when he called late the following evening to discuss setting an exit time frame for their case. "I've been thinking the same thing for a while," she disclosed, slightly uneasy with her confession.

"Are you sure?"

"Very—I need to think about my happiness, and what that looks like." As much as Colbie didn't like to admit such a thing, there was no disputing her life hadn't been fulfilling for a long time.

You see, when Colbie Colleen tried to fill her heart and soul with something designed to ease her personal pain, she didn't take into consideration doing so would remove what she loved most—sharing her accomplishments with someone who loved her for her intuitive abilities, not in spite of them. Yes, there were some who captured her interest more than others, but no one compared to who and what she lost . . .

No one could replace Brian.

Yet, when Decklin Kilgarry understood, her heart fluttered a little, igniting something she hadn't experienced for years. So much so, in fact, she wasn't sure she should continue working with him.

"How about if we talk about this tomorrow," Decklin suggested, knowing there was a possibility she could change her mind. So, with Colbie's agreeing to touch base the following day, they clicked off, each thinking of what was possibly in their futures.

Curling up on her hotel couch, Colbie switched on the news, then tucked a pillow under her head, only to awaken hours later to flashing from the television screen alerting viewers of breaking news. Instantly, she snatched her cell from the end table as she forced herself awake, then tapped a speed dial number. "Did you hear," she asked, her voice calm, but excited.

"Hear what?"

"Gloria Fuentes—she's unresponsive in ICU, but they're not saying what happened."

"Who's not saying?" Decklin sat up, checking the clock on his nightstand. "Do you realize it's one in the morning?"

"I'm sorry," Colbie chuckled, "but, you know I'm really not." She paused, momentarily wondering if he were upset because of the time.

A moment to gather himself. "Okay, I'm awake now—so, who's not saying what happened?"

"The late-night news—it was on the bottom scroll. She was found unconscious, and it doesn't look good. That's all I know . . ."

Decklin was quiet as he processed what Colbie told him, wondering who wanted to shut Gloria's mouth permanently, as well as how the press got wind of it so fast. "What are you thinking?"

"Right now, I'm not sure—but, I'm feeling as if it's some sort of challenge. What kind of challenge, I'm not sure . . ."

As much as Decklin wanted to know more, it wasn't the time. "Well, one thing's for sure—we won't know anything until later today."

"Longer than that, I'm guessing . . ."

Then, a brief silence as both wondered the same thing. "Breakfast in the morning," Colbie finally asked, somewhat uncomfortable with her request.

Decklin smiled to himself, clearly understanding their relationship was taking a turn. "Send me a text about when and where . . ."

CHAPTER 23

Though it had been several weeks since Analena Cortina ordered Decklin Kilgarry to bring to her the person who killed her husband, Analena's expectations hadn't changed—and, she wasn't shy about saying so when she met Amelia Sandoval for breakfast at their favorite South Beach bistro. But, it wasn't until both had a few Bloody Mary's under their belts did conversation turn to elements of just revenge.

"Whoever murdered my husband will pay," Analena declared again, causing the server to hesitate before approaching their table.

Watching carefully before answering, it wasn't until she headed to another table did Amelia continue the conversation. "Oh, please—everyone knows you and Hector weren't simpatico any longer, so I don't see the point of carrying on such a charade . . ."

A viable point.

Certainly, Analena was entitled to a hefty sum from life insurance and whatever else Hector squirreled away, so why was she so hell bent on learning who offed her husband?

"Justice," Analena confessed, though Amelia wasn't buying it for one second.

Time to pivot. "I understand—but, what I really want to know is who was with you the other day when you were out shopping? I saw you come out of a store empty-handed . . ."

"On Ocean Drive?"

A nod as Amelia took a bite of her salad. "She looked familiar, but I couldn't really get a good look . . ."

"Oh! You must mean Maria!" Analena smiled at the thought of her new friend. "I haven't known her for long, but I really like her . . ."

A new friend? As Amelia listened to Analena blather on about Maria, it was clear something was off. "What's her last name? Maybe I know her!"

"Valdez."

How did you meet?"

"Well, I admit it was a little weird—it was at Hector's memorial service. She came up to me and said she knew Hector from long ago—when they were children in Cuba—and, when she heard of his passing, she thought she should pay respects."

"That was nice of her," Amelia agreed, though she knew better—and, of course, since Hector was forever spending time in the mausoleum, confirming Maria's claim would be impossible.

With suspicion firmly planted, their remaining time together consisted of nothing more than small talk until they were about to part ways. "Why don't you, Maria and I get together for lunch next week," Amelia suggested. "I'd love to meet her!"

Somewhat startled, Analena turned to Amelia before heading to her car. "Why?"

Good question.

"Because I feel alone after Thomas died—and, it seems as if old friends aren't getting in touch like they did used to." A pause, hoping her words didn't sound like bullshit. "Maybe you're feeling the same thing . . ."

Analena smiled, her eyes filled with understanding. "I'll ask her," she promised, a new lilt in her voice. "In fact, we have Social Hour next week—she can be my guest, and that'll give you two a little time to get to know each other!"

A good idea?

Doubtful.

By midmorning, a relentless, grey fog cloaked Miami's beaches, putting the kibosh on most outdoor activities—but, for Colbie and Decklin?

A welcomed change.

"As much as I enjoy Florida," Colbie commented as Decklin pulled out her chair, "it's nice to have a cool, cozy day once in a while."

"Agreed—but, I have to admit I miss the seasons."

A smile. "Well, you haven't been here long enough to experience anything but hot, but I know what you mean. There are days I long for Seattle . . ."

As much as both would've enjoyed a leisurely late breakfast recalling memories, it wasn't to be. "I'm guessing you watched the news this morning," Colbie commented without looking up from her menu. "I'm going all out—pancakes and eggs for me!"

With their orders soon in the hands of their server, wishful thinking tipped into work. "To answer your question," Decklin replied, "I listened to the news while I brewed coffee. "

"Good—and, I had an early-morning discussion with the powers that be, and the consensus is Gloria was a hit job."

Decklin was quiet as he scanned the restaurant, taking note of everyone. "Exactly what I think—and, the fact Devon is lying in a hospital room because of having the shit kicked out of him is particularly concerning."

Colbie nodded her thanks as the server delivered their coffees and juice, then left them to their conversation. "I know—that's been on my mind. My gut tells me things are coming to a boiling point . . ."

"So, where does that leave us?"

"Well, I think we have a couple of choices—we can either wait to see what happens, or we can stir the pot a little."

"And, just what do you mean by 'stir the pot?'"

"The Social Hour—we got wind there's going to be a gathering on Friday, and it might be a good time to see how temperatures have changed, if you know what I mean."

"I do—I'm guessing that means you're going to attend?"

Colbie nodded, taking her time to answer. "I am—and, if you're up for it, so are you. You can come as my guest . . ."

While the idea held promise, Decklin wasn't thrilled with it. "I don't know, Colbie—Analena and Amelia Sandoval will undoubtedly be there. I've already met them, so I doubt it will take long to figure out why I'm there."

"I thought of that—I think the only way we can pull it off is to let them know you're going to be there in your official capacity. Analena asked you to find out who killed her husband, so it's natural for you to attend—and, I suspect Amelia will honor a request to not say anything to the contrary . . ."

"I get it—but, there's certainly an element of risk. With losing two members of their Social Hour, how many are left other than Analena and Amelia?"

"Several—and, yes, it's narrowed down somewhat, but I think Hector and Thomas will be replaced quickly. And, we still have Aiden Lopez on our radar—we can't forget that."

So, by the time Decklin and Colbie took their last sips of coffee, while each felt a bit uncertain about their Social Hour plans, both felt attending the Friday night soirée was a must.

The whole thing was iffy, though . . .

After a few days in the hospital under his belt, Devon was released, eager to get back to work—something causing Decklin more than a little concern. "Don't show your face at the office until next week," he ordered, as he adjusted his cell phone volume.

"But . . ."

"No! I need you in top working order so we can be done with this case as soon as possible."

"I feel fine! Just a little black and blue is all . . ."

"Well . . ."

Suddenly, Devon appeared at Decklin's office door, smirking, cell up to his ear. "I'll take that as a yes!"

"What the hell . . ." Then, a gut laugh. "You got me!"

Oddly, Devon's surprise appearance was exactly what both needed, each one feeling the weight of their case needing to lift. "Now, get your ass in here, and let's get to work!"

Relieved to be back on track, Decklin and Devon discussed plans for the Friday night Social Hour, Decklin suggesting Devon surveil, inconspicuously taking photos of everyone attending. "And, I'll be wired—that way, you can talk to me and listen to conversations, but I won't speak directly to you."

"That's doable" Devon agreed. "But, we only have two days."

"That's where you come in—how do you feel about taking the lead to set everything up? You know, equipment and making sure it works . . ."

"I'm in. I'll need to meet you to get you wired, though—and, what about Colbie? Do you want her wired, too?"

Decklin smiled, knowing it would be interesting to watch Colbie in action. "Oh, she'll be wired, alright! But in a different way . . ."

CHAPTER 24

As much as Decklin didn't enjoy formal attire, when he picked Colbie up at her hotel, he started liking it a lot more. "You look absolutely fantastic," he commented as he held the passenger's door open for her.

"Thank you, Sir—as do you. But, I'm still not sure about our arriving together. Maybe . . ."

"Wait—are you suggesting Anderson should drop you off?"

"Well . . ."

Exactly what Decklin didn't want to hear—and, if he were honest with himself, arriving separately would spoil the evening. Of course, he didn't want to admit it, but stepping out with Colbie made him feel alive—something he hadn't felt for quite some time. "Well, I think it makes sense we arrive together since I'm your guest—otherwise, it would seems awkward."

Colbie smiled, noticing Decklin's eyes lingered as she gracefully folded her legs into the sedan. "You're right! I don't know what I was thinking . . ."

His smile matching hers, he closed the door then climbed in behind the wheel. "So, what's our story? People will wonder who I am—and, by the way, I contacted Analena and Amelia to let them know I'm going to be there under the auspices of learning who murdered their husbands."

"Excellent. So, how about if we tell them we're long-time friends, and you're in Florida seeking real estate investments? It sounds generic enough, and I doubt it will raise suspicion, especially Aidan's."

"Works for me," Decklin acknowledged, glancing at his watch. "We're going to meet Devon around the corner from Aidan's, so he can get us wired—he said he got the most indiscreet, powerful surveillance equipment he could find."

So, thirty minutes later with wires planted and plans in place, Decklin Kilgarry and Colbie Colleen arrived at Aidan Lopez's front door looking every bit the power couple. "Are you ready for our performance," Colbie asked as she heard Aidan's footsteps on the foyer's marble floor.

"I confess it's not my strong suit . . ."

Sensing Decklin's discomfort, Colbie squeezed his hand. "Don't worry—I'll take care of you!"

It was interesting how Gloria Fuentes's medical episode was swept under the media rug as if outlets were afraid to dig into reasons why she wound up comatose in intensive care. But, if Gloria had anything to say about it, staying out of the public eye was fine with her. In fact, after opening her eyes during the wee hours on the day of Aidan Lopez's Social Hour, her first directive was 'no visitors.' Knowing that, one could only speculate the reason why—was it because she was embarrassed by her appearance?

Doubtful.

Gloria just didn't want to draw attention to the cartel due to the revenge she knew she must enact.

As she lay in her hospital bed, there was little doubt she was the target of a hit—the question was who decided to pull the figurative trigger? One of her own? Or, a different cartel jockeying for position?

Perhaps someone else.

Unfortunately, Gloria could well imagine some of her own organization members being stupid enough to try such a thing. After all, the majority of them weren't accepted into the cartel based on intellectual prowess. Not only that, most were followers rather than leaders, something playing well for Gloria after her father's passing.

Granted, she hadn't enjoyed the trust of cartel peons as her father did, but she truly didn't think it was necessary— he was dead, and she wasn't. Still, no matter how she rationalized her first few months as the new cartel queen, she knew trouble would soon brew when choosing a more hands-on approach.

Apparently, it already had.

Of course, when nurses discovered Gloria was awake, a flurry of activity prevented her from making plans—and, it wasn't until later that day she learned the reason for her current situation. "You're saying I was bitten by a coral snake," she asked, glaring at the nurse who delivered the news.

"That's what it says here—but, if you have any questions, you can ask your doctor when he does rounds." Then, the nurse was gone, leaving Gloria to think. Plot.

Decide.

"Colbie! How nice to see you again!" Aidan Lopez extended his hand, giving Decklin the once over as he invited them in. Another proposed handshake directed at Decklin. "I'm Aidan Lopez—welcome to my home!"

Accepting the gesture while introducing himself, Decklin hoped he wasn't staring as Aidan led them from the foyer to a private room the size of small gymnasium. Appointed with treasures from the art deco era, money dripped from artwork on the walls, soft lighting accentuating each. "It feels like a speakeasy in here," Decklin commented under his breath as their host approached guests who arrived before them.

Naturally, there were introductions.

Luckily, it didn't take long for Decklin to step into his role as a real estate magnate, listening to everyone he met, quickly assessing his first impressions. Parting from Colbie, each set their marks, Colbie soon tuning in to those who captured her attention.

But, it wasn't until Gisele Escalante waltzed into the room did the energy change.

Dressed to kill, she was fluid and graceful as she crossed the room to greet Aidan, thanking him for inviting her. "You're always welcome in my home," he promised, slipping a pudgy arm around her waist.

With radar in gear, Colbie watched, paying particular attention to how others in the Social Hour group accepted someone so . . . different. Most figured, of course, Gisele was nothing more than Aidan's employee, showing her little more than obligated attention.

And, Colbie was certain Gisele noticed.

It wasn't long, however, until Colbie caught the scent of energy changing, Gisele offering something more familiar than the rest of the guests. Tuning in, Colbie felt a seeping anger from the high priestess, cueing her that Aidan's operations manager was attending the cocktail party for reasons other than having a good time.

Decklin noticed the shift, too—though he hadn't met Gisele in person, he suspected she chose to live among the shadows when living her private life.

Catching Colbie's attention with a slight nod, Decklin crossed the room to her, standing beside her as she visited with two bankers from South Beach. Briefly, she introduced him, both soon politely excusing themselves after a short, meaningless conversation.

Distancing themselves, Decklin and Colbie chatted as old friends usually do, laughing and sipping, no one the wiser regarding the pair's true intent for attending—until Gisele suddenly appeared at Colbie's side. "Interesting group, isn't it," she asked, keeping her eyes on the petite redhead.

An engaging smile. "It's fun to see how the other side lives, that's for sure!" A quick glance at Aidan. "What brings you here? Is there something I should know?"

"Other than I never mix business with pleasure?" Of course, it was a barbed question, Gisele delivering it with precision.

When thinking about it, though, Gisele's starting a conversation with Colbie probably wasn't such a hot idea. Since Gisele was completely aware of the reason Colbie was in Miami, it did seem a rather strange approach.

Picking up on the edge in Gisele's voice, it seemed ruffled feathers needed to be smoothed. "I meant no offense, Gisele. I'm sorry . . ."

Then, a smile. "None taken—I'm here because Aidan asked me to attend, and I couldn't say no." Gisele scanned the room, then focused again on Colbie. "I'm curious why you're here, though . . ."

As she spoke, she felt Decklin place his hand at the small of her back—a protection of sorts. "Well, as you probably know, I, too, don't mix business with pleasure. Decklin and I are old friends and, when Aidan invited me . . . well, I wanted them to meet."

Her eyes assessing Decklin, Gisele again smiled. "Just friends?"

Before Colbie could answer, Gisele excused herself, pleased she attended the Social Hour. If she hadn't?

She never would've suspected Colbie Colleen was one to keep within her sight. The more she kept an eye on her, she knew . . .

Something just wasn't right.

So, with suspicions in full swing on more than one front, that's the way it went at the Social Hour gathering until Analena Cortina arrived with her guest. Though it was more important to introduce Maria Valdez to the moneymakers, Analena was thoughtful enough to take a few seconds of Decklin's time to do the same.

Though the introduction was short, it was enough to arouse his suspicion and, as Maria worked the room, an uncomfortable energy settled. Surreptitiously keeping a keen eye on each guest, Decklin and Colbie arrived at the same conclusion.

Maria Valdez wasn't who she professed to be.

Two hours into his surveillance and listening intently to Decklin's and Colbie's conversations, Devon began to think he wasn't ready to assume his full-time, investigative responsibilities. Closing his eyes more than once to will away pain, it wasn't until he heard Decklin's response to meeting Maria Valdez did he realize the timbre of his partner's voice changed. *What's that all about,* he wondered as he increased the volume in his headset a few clicks. But, since Analena's introduction was brief, there was little time to get a take on anything concrete.

He did find it interesting, though, that a new player was suddenly on their radar, causing him to question why Maria's name never came up in conversation with anyone, especially Analena. Devon considered it weird at the least, prompting him to make a note to research her name the following day. *Probably a shot in the dark,* he thought as Social Hour guests began to depart.

Training high tech binos on everyone as they headed to their vehicles, one person in particular caught his eye. *Who the hell is that?* Recognizing the woman as the one he saw with Analena a few days prior, it was then he knew something was up . . .

Something worth investigating.

As often happens with hospital stays, it wasn't until the following day did Gloria Fuentes have the opportunity to grill her doctor about the reason she was there. After providing a full assessment of what happened as well as her current health, Gloria's true nature decided to emerge, excoriating the physician for something that wasn't his fault. Gratitude?

In short supply.

THE SOCIAL HOUR 233
A Decklin Kilgarry Mystery—Book 4

Demanding an immediate release that was against the doctor's recommendations, after calling her top operative to pick her up, Gloria was unceremoniously wheeled out to a waiting black sedan. Dismissing the nurse without a thank you, Manuel opened the car door for her, wisely not mentioning Gloria's drooping eye and labored breathing. Instead, he took the more compassionate approach, offering to hang around as her security guy until she was looking and feeling better.

Something Gloria promptly refused.

Figuring it would only be a day or two until she was back to her queenie self, it seemed prudent to use the time for careful planning. In her mind, there was only one person who could've pulled off such a thing . . .

One who deserved to die.

Deciding to meet early the following morning after the Social Hour gathering, Decklin, Devon, and Colbie were armed with coffee and bagels by eight-thirty. "Good call with the bagels," Colbie commented as she spread cream cheese to the edges of each half. "Breakfast is my favorite meal . . ."

Smiling, Decklin snagged a bagel of his own, noticing Devon opted for coffee only. "Okay—who wants to go first," he asked, making sure his notepad was turned to a fresh page.

Since Devon wasn't eating, it made sense for him to kick off their meeting. "Of course, I recorded the entire event—but, there was one person who really caught my interest."

"Name?"

"Maria Valdez . . ." Devon paused, thinking if Decklin and Colbie agreed, there was something to investigate. "I find it interesting, she wasn't on our radar, at all—especially after all the conversations we had with Analena. Maria's name didn't come up . . ."

"There was something familiar about her, too," Decklin offered, "and I felt as if I'd seen her before."

"Was she the one with the long black hair," Devon asked, making sure they were talking about the same person.

Colbie nodded, finishing chewing before she answered. "Yep—and, I wondered about her as well." A quick glance at Decklin. "I didn't mention it last night, figuring we'd hack through everything this morning."

"That makes sense," Decklin agreed before returning his attention to Devon. "Did you happen to do any research on her before now?"

"Yes, but I didn't find anything concrete—I couldn't find anyone matching our Maria Valdez. On social media, there were many by the same name—however, I'm positive she's the woman I saw with Analena on Ocean Drive."

Decklin scribbled a few notes, then focused on Colbie. "And, what about you—what are your thoughts on the evening? Who captured your attention?"

"Two people—the rest of them were nothing but social climbers, there for the single reason of making it into digital society pages." Colbie sat back in her chair, then took a sip of coffee. "Aidan was as charming as he was the first time

I attended, and there were a few whom I didn't recognize." When Gisele Escalante walked in, though, I admit I did a double take . . ."

"I know—that surprised me, too. Do you have any feelings about why she was there?"

"Though I've had minimal, personal contact with Gisele regarding our case, it was easy to pick up on her overall vibe—and, it wasn't pleasant."

Decklin was quiet for a few moments as he cycled through their previous conversations regarding the Santeria high priestess. "I guess that really doesn't surprise me, since you've been having doubts about her recently."

"Agreed—my antennae are up. I suspected she's playing both sides of the fence, and last night makes me think I'm on the right track."

"But, why," Devon asked, his expression signaling it didn't make sense to him.

"That's the thing, isn't it," Colbie responded, smiling. "That's exactly what we need to figure out . . ."

Listening carefully, Decklin had a question of his own. "Well, let's get down to it—what do you think right now? Without having additional information . . ."

Another sip. "There's little doubt Gisele is a powerful woman, no matter the circle—she's comfortable in her role as Aidan's top executive at the shipping company, and she's equally as comfortable in her own skin as a Santeria high priestess. There's definitely a duplicity associated with her, and that makes her particularly dangerous."

"In what way," Devon asked, hoping he didn't sound like an idiot.

"Well, I think we first look at Gisele's past, as well as what we already know . . ."

"We know she's from Cuba, and she's worked for the U.S. for years," Devon offered.

"Good—what else?" While it appeared Colbie was asking for opinions, she really thought it was a good time for Devon to learn how to dissect a case, person by person.

"Well, she's obviously involved in a dark, deeply-steeped religion stemming from her time in Cuba." Devon paused as he cycled through possibilities in his mind. "Do you think they're related? Her involvement with the shipping company, I mean . . ."

As Decklin listened, a new picture began forming, one placing Gisele Escalante in his crosshairs. "Of course, they are—the Santeria gig is the perfect disguise to carry out something nefarious. It allows her to carry on two lives . . ."

"Yes," Colbie agreed. "But, I think it goes deeper than that—we also need to consider a few others, though. Until we do that, we can't consider Gisele specifically until we rule out everyone else. If Gisele is the one left standing, we have our suspect . . ."

Again, Devon looked slightly confused. "Just so I'm sure, why—and, what—are we accusing her of?"

Decklin focused on him, knowing he was feeling a little lost. "Correct me if I'm wrong, Colbie, but are we beginning to dial in on who murdered Thomas Sandoval and Hector Cortina . . ."

"Correct," Colbie replied. "And, while I was tuning in on Gisele at the Social Hour, I began to understand who's her true target. I had a vision of three things—a snake, a voodoo doll, and a tattooed foot."

"Seriously? I get the voodoo stuff is tied to Gisele—the snake, too?"

"Yes—but, when I had a vision of hospital monitors, everything began coming into focus."

"Gloria Fuentes?"

"Yep—and, it's common knowledge on my end that Gloria Fuentes has a snake tattooed on her right foot."

"Okay—two suspects. Do you think Gisele is responsible for Gloria's winding up in the hospital?"

"Maybe—but, there's also been chatter about dissension among cartel members after Gloria assumed the top dog position. After her father died, there's more than one who isn't pleased with the way she's running the operation."

"Because she's a woman," Decklin asked, though he was ninety-nine percent certain that was the reason.

"Yes—there are a few old-timers in the cartel who were fiercely connected to Juan, and they view Gloria's methods as treasonous . . ."

Decklin and Devon were silent as Colbie spoke, both recognizing they were whittling down their suspect list to two. But, what Colbie told them next blew them out of the water. "There's one person on Gisele's radar—someone who can take her down."

"Who," Decklin and Devon asked in unison.

"Me."

CHAPTER 25

Some things in life simply need to be done by the person most attached to the situation—which is why Gloria Fuentes decided to take care of business herself based on her father's sage advice. "My dear daughter," he said in a moment of private conversation, "when the situation calls for truth, allow history to be your guide."

Of course, at the time, Gloria really didn't have any idea of what he was talking about since she was only sixteen. But, at that moment?

She understood every word.

Even though she gave Aidan Lopez the benefit of the doubt, the facts could no longer be ignored—rightfully earned cartel money was being skimmed. After careful review, there was no one else who could carry off such a thing, though her suspicions-turned-fact didn't include the man in charge. In fact, she suspected Aidan didn't have a damned thing to do with it.

In Gloria's mind, the suspect was obvious—Gisele Escalante was responsible, though Gloria couldn't prove it. *Who needs proof,* Gloria asked herself as she began to plan her next move. After all, who else would've implemented a plan against her that included a coral snake? *It's right up your alley, Gisele . . .*

And, it was, too.

Snakes and Santeria seemed a perfect marriage and, as far as Gloria knew, there wasn't anyone close to her who would think of such a thing—mainly because they weren't that bright. Not to mention most of them would shoot a snake upon first sight before depositing it in someone's bed to do the deadly deed.

An erroneous assumption?

Possibly.

Decklin and Devon said nothing, both trying to digest the bombshell Colbie just dropped. Eyeing her carefully, Decklin didn't recognize an ounce of fear or mild trepidation—it was merely a fact needing careful attention.

"Just to make sure I understand—you're saying Gisele has you in her crosshairs?"

"Yes."

It was then Decklin realized something interesting—he wasn't upset because of his professional connection to Colbie. It was his personal connection, and that was something he didn't care to admit—to Colbie or himself. After a failed marriage and one doomed, significant relationship, the last thing he needed in his life was complications.

But, there it was.

Colbie's admission hit home in a way making him uncharacteristically uncomfortable, yet it was something he needed to address—not to her, but himself. The best way to resolve such a thing?

Confronting it head on.

"I confess there's a reason I asked you to dinner," Decklin began as he and Colbie settled into a booth at a steakhouse she mentioned months prior. "Something I couldn't discuss in our meeting with Devon this morning . . ."

"That sounds ominous . . ."

"I guess that depends on how you look at it," Decklin replied, smiling. "I just need to be honest in all facets of our working together."

Colbie was quiet for a moment, realizing Decklin needed to address something serious. "Then, I suggest we order a cocktail and settle in . . ."

"Done!" Signaling their server, Decklin ordered two glasses of wine and a small appetizer. "I do better when I have food in front of me," he joked, hoping to alleviate the giant knot in his stomach. It had been a long time since he confessed feelings he carried below the surface. "Okay— when you were talking about Gisele making you her number one target, it raised a level of concern."

"You mean concern about the case?"

Decklin shook his head. "No—it was concern about you."

Colbie said nothing for a moment, unsure if she wanted to have a conversation forcing her to deal with her own feelings. "Why are you concerned about me?"

Decklin inhaled, unaware he was holding his breath. "Because I'm beginning to consider you a part of my personal life . . ."

A slow exhale.

Actually, when he heard the words come out of his mouth, they didn't sound as bad as he anticipated. "When we began working together," he continued, "I slowly began to realize we not only worked well together, but there was a degree of comfort I haven't experienced for quite a while. At least since Cecily left, and probably before . . ."

Colbie said nothing, fully aware of how difficult it was to admit he had feelings for her. "Well, I don't really know what to say . . ."

"I know! It's inappropriate given our working together— and, if you prefer to pull the plug, I completely understand.

After all, you didn't sign on—"

A smile. "May I say something, please?"

Decklin blushed, hoping she didn't notice. "Of course!"

Colbie took a sip of her merlot, then placed the glass on the table and leaned forward, looking squarely into his eyes. "I've been feeling the same thing . . ."

Stunned silence.

"If you remember, I spilled my guts when we talked weeks ago—you know, about my work."

"And, Brian," Decklin commented softly. "I know that was difficult for you to do . . ."

"It was—but, by doing so I came to realize I can't keep holding Brian up as my hands-off flag, if you know what I mean."

"I don't think you were—"

"Yes, I was—and, when I realized it, I also realized I wasn't being fair to myself. So, I had a decision to make— open myself up to the uncertainty of something new, or stay buried in a hole, refusing to let someone in."

Another sip.

"So, the way I see it, we're both in the same boat!"

Laughing Decklin popped a stuffed mushroom in his mouth, then sat back, feeling a sense of ease for the first time that evening. "So, Ms. Colleen, where do we go from here?"

"Good question—but, for now, I think our first priority has to be our case. Everything's coming to a head, and it's going to be sooner than later when it breaks loose . . ."

"What about you? If Gisele is gunning for you, it's a threat we can't take lightly."

Prophetic words, indeed . . .

There's one thing Gloria Fuentes wanted everyone within her organization to know—she was a woman of her word. So, when her best operative wound up in a back alley with two bullets in the back of his head, those prone to questions decided to keep their traps shut.

Probably best.

Everyone, of course, knew who took him out, none wanting to confront Manuel's killer—and, really, they couldn't blame her. Always bad-mouthing Fuentes behind her back, it was only a matter of time until Gloria took her just revenge.

She was, however, a bit surprised to learn it was Manuel who released the coral snake into her bed hoping to effect another personnel change. But, since Gloria ordered a similar technique at Gisele's home only weeks prior, using Manuel as the fall guy, it made sense he'd try the same with her.

Again, not the brightest.

Gloria had to admit sending Manuel to Gisele's home late that night was a risk—at most, it relayed the message of

Gloria's knowing Gisele was siphoning cartel money, an act placing Gisele in Gloria's line of fire.

But, when word circled back to her that Manual was making plans, plotting her demise? There was only one solution . . .

Traitor down.

After a meager, short, and tepid investigation, Florida's authorities chose to look the other way, figuring they had more important things to do other than press cartel members for information. All were liars, so there was really no point—a decision further emboldening the cartel queen.

So, with Manuel taken care of and knowing she must deal with Gisele Escalante personally, Gloria decided a simple bullet to the brain wasn't as dramatic as she desired. However, carrying out such a hit proved more difficult than she thought. *It requires careful planning*, she told herself, knowing she could trust no one to help. Unfortunately, taking extra time to solidify plans probably wasn't in her best interest since it allowed the high priestess an opportunity to hatch a plot of her own.

So . . .

There was a reason Gisele reached the highest position within her Santeria culture—her intuitive abilities were on par with Colbie Colleen's, and Gisele wasn't afraid to use them. But, it wasn't until after the Social Hour gathering she had a decision to make, basing it on who was most important. *I can deal with Gloria later,* she finally decided, officially placing the cartel queen on the back burner as she extracted the voodoo doll she fashioned nearly two weeks prior from her altar drawer.

Wheels in motion.

As Decklin and Colbie left the steakhouse, Decklin placed his hand on her back as they stepped onto the sidewalk. "Promise me you'll keep your eyes peeled," he requested as Anderson pulled up to the curb.

"I promise—and, after we put this case to bed, I think we need to pick up our conversation. Until then, however, it's more important to take down Thomas's and Hector's killer."

"You're certain they're one and the same?"

"Without a doubt—and, I feel as if we'll have our answer soon."

So, with that, they parted, each thinking about what they had to accomplish—and, how they were going to deal with their personal feelings when it came time to part at the end of their case.

An end Colbie felt was just around the corner.

CHAPTER 26

"Anderson, will you please drop me off at the beach—you know, where Decklin and I met at the beginning of our working together?"

"It's dark, Colbie—I don't think that's particularly wise."

Sighing, Colbie agreed. "I know—but, I have some thinking to do, and I don't feel like being cooped up in my hotel room to do it. I promise I won't be long! Besides, you'll be there . . ."

Knowing he could say nothing to dissuade her, Anderson complied, arriving at the private beach within twenty. "Take this," he advised, handing Colbie a walkie. "If you see anything . . . channel two."

"Thanks—but, I'll only be about twenty minutes. As I said, I just need to clear my head a bit . . ." Grabbing her service revolver, she tucked it into her left coat pocket, a small flashlight in the right. *You never know,* she thought as she exited the SUV.

So, with that, Colbie left Anderson, opting to navigate the private trail by moonlight rather than use the flashlight. Spying the familiar bench, she sat, listening to waves as memories claimed her. *I'm sorry, Brian,* she thought as she recycled her conversation with Decklin. *You'll always be in my heart—but, it's time for me to move on.*

As difficult as that realization was, Colbie knew it was her truth. If she had any chance at being happy, she had to let go of the pain and sorrow. *But, you know me—all you have to do is give me a sign, and I'll know you're with me. I guess I can't ask for more than that . . .*

With tears spilling, Colbie listened to waves lapping against the shore, wondering if she were doing the right thing—and, it was then a tiny, white feather fell onto her lap. *How lovely,* she thought, scanning the sky for the bird who lost it—but, there wasn't one.

It was then she knew.

"I'll always love you, Brian," she whispered as she rose, then made her way back up the trail.

But, as she reached the small, sandy pullout, she stopped, her intuition in high gear. Stepping back into the shadows, she scanned the parking lot, then focused on Anderson, his head resting on the headrest. *That's weird,* she thought, knowing he wouldn't be napping—it wasn't his style.

Again scanning the pullout, Colbie approached the black SUV, her gut telling her to take caution. Slowly, she inched toward the driver's door, noticing its panel was marked with a Santeria symbol—one dripping blood.

Shit! Instantly, she pulled her revolver from her pocket, training it on the SUV and, though Colbie didn't want to call attention to herself by using the flashlight, she had no choice. Shining it on the driver's window, she inched her way toward the SUV, gasping as she realized Anderson's head lolled lifelessly to the left, his throat slit from ear-to ear in a death smile.

But, before she could react, a wicked blow to the back of her head dropped her like a forty-pound sandbag, a chilling whisper in her ear as she crumpled to the ground.

Lights out.

Decklin checked his watch, surprised he hadn't heard from Colbie—but, by the time the following morning rolled around and he still hadn't heard from her, he decided to call.

Voicemail.

The same in the afternoon, too.

It wasn't until he learned of Anderson's murder on the evening news, a beach jogger finding his body in the SUV, dread coursed through him. *That's it! I'm calling,* he thought as he pulled out the piece of paper on which Colbie scribbled her handler's contact number.

No answer.

Odd, yet understandable, especially if they had little information.

Even so, it pissed him off.

Due to the sensitive nature of the victim, there was little available information from the media. *Time to circle the wagons*, he silently promised Colbie as he texted Devon with his concerns.

Within the hour, they sat in Decklin's living room reviewing every possibility. The only thing they knew, however, was what was reported on the news—and, that wasn't much for obvious reasons.

"The question is," Devon commented, "why in the hell was Anderson at that location in the first place?"

"That's what I want to know—granted, I don't know Miami as well as I should, but when I got a glimpse on the news, it looked familiar. Like I'd been there before . . ."

"Okay—let's go with that. Why did it look familiar?"

Decklin smiled, knowing he needed to let Devon take over as much as Decklin was willing to let him take the lead. A pair of fresh eyes never hurt anything, and it was prudent to make sure they weren't getting off track. "That's the thing," he replied. "The pullout reminded me of where Colbie and I met when we needed to have a conversation about the case. It was private, and I recall her telling me she got permission . . ."

"Was it a private pullout? Usually, a private beach is connected to someone's property—so, how did that work?"

"I don't know—we really didn't talk about it."

"Can you get there again?"

"I think so—but, you can bet it's going to be taped. Since Anderson worked for the Feds, it going to be impossible to access."

"So, what about getting eyes on it from a distance?"

"You mean a drone?"

Devon chuckled, surprised Decklin thought of it. "No— but, if we can get to a vantage point where we can see with high-tech binos, we can at least get an idea."

"Good thinking—the only problem is we don't have high-tech binos."

"Au contraire, my friend—what do you think I used when surveilling the Social Hour?"

Laughing, Decklin appreciated his partner more every minute. "How foolish of me not to know!"

Chuckling, Devon stood, pulling his car keys from his pocket. "Let's go! You can point me in the right direction . . ."

"I'm pretty sure it's close," Decklin commented as they tried to find a good spot to get eyes on the private beach parking area. "Due east . . ."

Devon fished out the binos from the center console, adjusting them for his eyes. "It's a lot smaller than I envisioned—but, I'm thinking if we go to the top floor of that commercial office building, we'll be in good shape."

Since Decklin didn't have a different idea, he agreed and, ten minutes later, they were in place, trying to make the most of the somewhat obscured view of the area. "Anderson's SUV is still there," Devon murmured as he trained the binos on the sandy pullout. "And, you were right. It's taped with authorities keeping guard . . ."

"Not for long, though—and, I'm kind of surprised they haven't taken the vehicle by now."

"How long does that usually take?"

"It varies—but, I guarantee it'll be gone soon. So, I think the best we can do is scan the area with your fancy binos to see if you can pick up on anything."

"Roger that . . ." But, as much as Devon tried to find something they could use, he came up with nothing.

"Okay—back to the drawing board. Let's head out before we arouse suspicion . . ."

Devon, however, wasn't quite ready to leave the only lead they had. "Just one more pass—if I don't see anything, we'll get out of here. Okay with you?" Before Decklin could answer, Devon suddenly stopped talking, thinking he spied something at the base of a palm tree. "What the hell is that," he murmured, keeping the binos trained on the tree.

"What do you see?"

"I don't know—but, it's something."

"Small enough for the Feds to miss it as they gather evidence?"

"No—I don't think so." Devon adjusted the binos slightly, attempting to zoom in more. "It's about four inches—maybe five."

"Clearly big enough for someone to see it—so, maybe it wasn't there when the Feds combed the scene for evidence."

"Or, they were completely inefficient," Devon replied. "But, it looks like a figure of some sort—light colored," Devon passed the binos to Decklin, keeping an eye on the tree. "It's the palm on the left—the one set back, closest to the beach."

After taking a few seconds to locate the tree, Decklin had to agree. "It has arms and legs—and, one of it's eyes is missing. There's an 'x' in place of the left eye . . ."

Suddenly, Devon blanched, color draining from his face as he realized what they were seeing. "Deck—I think that's a voodoo thing!"

"You mean like a voodoo doll?"

"Exactly! When I was doing research on Santeria, there were tons of images of them."

After a few moments to digest what Devon told him, Decklin knew instantly where they needed to go next. "C'mon," he ordered as he bolted toward the elevator. "Move your ass!"

CHAPTER 27

"Check the navigation system," Decklin ordered as he headed south on the A1A. "The route will be there from when I surveilled Gisele . . ."

Deftly, Devon brought up what they needed to know. "We're approaching our target from a different direction, but once you reach South Beach, we're in good shape." A glance at Decklin. "So, do you want to tell me what you're thinking?"

"I'm positive Gisele has Colbie—and, Gisele's responsible for everything. Thomas Sandoval. Hector. And, now, she set her sights on the only person who can ruin her . . ."

Devon was quiet, thinking of their meeting the previous day. "She said that was going to happen . . ."

"I know—and, she said everything was going to come to a head soon."

Devon nodded, then focused on lights from buildings as they sped past, knowing Decklin needed to concentrate on their mission. The truth was walking into something dangerous never entered his mind when Decklin proposed the idea of becoming business partners.

In a way, he wished it had.

As if reading his partner's mind, Decklin knew how he was feeling. "We have to be smarter than Gisele," he advised, knowing they couldn't bust down the door with guns blazing. "She's not the woman people think she is, and that makes her even more dangerous . . ."

"Meaning?"

"She's cunning—and, that's the worst kind of criminal. It's one thing to pursue someone escaped from prison because authorities know what to expect, always planning for the worst." Decklin paused as he exited the highway, then headed to the part of South Beach most chose to ignore. "That type of criminal is predictable, and Gisele Escalante is anything but . . ."

"I agree. We really don't have any idea of what she's going to do, or what she's capable of . . ."

"Exactly." As Decklin headed south, both were aware of a change in the evening air. The energy. Within minutes, the swampy wetlands rose to meet them, eye shine of a gator glinting on the side of the road as they passed.

"This place gives me the creeps," Devon confessed as Decklin slowed when lights from a small cabin came into distant view. "Seriously? This is where she lives," Devon asked as Decklin cut the engine and headlights.

"It is . . ."

For a moment, both sat in silence, each scanning the area. "Do you think she knows we're coming for her," Devon eventually whispered, as if Gisele could hear.

"I don't know—but, my gut tells me the voodoo doll wasn't left purposely at the base of that palm tree."

"You mean you think Gisele dropped it?"

Decklin was quiet for a moment, thinking. "Maybe—or, she could've had someone involved in the Santeria cult help her, and that person dropped it. "

When thinking about it, both scenarios were plausible, and the fact Colbie Colleen was petite gave anyone wanting to harm her an advantage. "Do you think Colbie was armed," Devon asked, envisioning the worst.

"I don't know—we never discussed it, and we really had no reason to. Don't forget, it was only yesterday we learned Gisele had Colbie on her radar . . ."

"She seemed pretty positive about it, that's for sure . . ."

Parked on the side of the road, their black sedan blended in with midnight's ink, allowing Decklin and Devon to remain unnoticed as they crafted their next move. "Candles are burning," Decklin observed, their flames' flickering within the cabin as if attempting to soften the reason he and Devon were there. "Let's use that to our advantage . . ."

"How?"

Decklin glanced at each side of the cabin. "Obviously, we need to approach from the dark side." Then, a question

Devon thought he'd never hear. "Do you have your weapon?"

Then, an answer Devon never thought he'd say. "Yep."

Taking a few minutes to discuss strategy, the two men exited the sedan, using shadows at the swamp's edge for cover. Creeping toward the window located on the left side of the cabin and using hand signals, Decklin motioned for Devon to take his position on the far side of the window, while he assumed his on the side closest to the porch. Their first concern?

The window was open.

Peering in from the side, Decklin scanned the room, instantly locating Colbie—wrists and ankles zip tied, her chin rested at the base of her throat. Again, he signaled Devon, his fingers in a vertical 'v.'

Target located.

To Colbie's right was a small table with three candles dripping wax onto its surface, as well as a syringe illuminated by their flickering. Propped against the vial was a photo of Colbie, each eye replaced with an 'x.'

Behind her, a closed door.

Knowing Gisele had to be near, Decklin motioned to Devon, signaling it was time to approach the door on the porch—a much more difficult task since it was slightly illuminated against the blue-black, murky swamp. Glancing at Devon, Decklin hesitated, knowing his partner's arm could be an issue, though Devon previously commented it was much better. Still, Decklin considered moving in by himself. Pointing to his partner's arm, Devon shook his head emphatically, then pointed toward the cabin.

Stealthy and silent, only croaking frogs masked their sound as they moved into position to the sides of the screen door, well aware alerting Gisele could be Colbie's death knell. With weapons still drawn, each listened for an indication Gisele was in the room, Decklin quickly determining she wasn't . . .

Until the door behind Colbie opened.

Her robe's white fabric in stark contrast to the night's jet black, Gisele entered the room, her head covered by a white keel. In her hands, she carried two brown vials and small scissors, placing them on the square table.

Taking the syringe in her slender fingers, she carefully inserted the needle into one vial, drawing its liquid. Then, the second. "It's really a shame," Gisele suddenly commented as Colbie looked up, instantly recognizing what was about to happen, "I have to take such precautions . . ."

"Precautions for what," Colbie asked calmly, Decklin immediately recognizing what a pro she truly was. Keeping his eyes on her, he felt her resolve.

Her courage.

Gisele stopped mid-draw, as if Colbie's question were in some way offensive. Ignoring it, she continued what she was about to say. "In many ways, I consider you my equal— which, unfortunately, makes you an unacceptable part of my life."

"If you're talking about my figuring out it was you who murdered Thomas Sandoval and Hector Cortina, I guess you'd be correct. Were they, too, an unacceptable aspect of your life?"

A soft chuckle. "Yes—but, both got what they deserved."

Though Colbie didn't show it, she thought she heard something on the porch as Gisele extracted the needle from the second vial, cocking her head toward the door as if she, too, heard something unusual. Crossing to the screen door, she peered into the swamp, assessing, then returned to Colbie, the syringe held gracefully in her fingers. "Why did they deserve to die," Colbie asked, hoping to swivel Gisele's attention back to their conversation.

Without answering, Gisele placed the syringe on the table, snipped the zip tie, then grabbed Colbie's arm roughly, searching for a vein. "Because," she finally answered, "both were traitors to our homeland."

"Cuba?"

"You know the answer to that—and, you also know Thomas and Hector were crossing to the other side of the street." A pause. "Of course, I knew that, and when I figured out both were selling out my country to the Mexican cartel and the States, I simply couldn't tolerate it any longer."

"So, you took matters into your own hands . . ."

"Well, someone had to—and, the obvious solution was me."

Colbie didn't flinch as Gisele flicked the veins in her right arm sharply to make them rise. "So, you killed two men because they dared to do the same thing you do . . ."

A stunned look. "What I do?"

"Well, of course—you accuse your victims of duplicity, yet you're doing the same thing. You're just as guilty as they are, and I'm fairly certain Aidan has no idea of what you're up to. But, I doubt he'd be accepting—so, how is what you're doing any different? You're selling out my country to Cuba, are you not? The country that pays you handsomely?"

As Decklin and Devon listened, both recognized Colbie was buying time, the conversation directed toward Gisele, forcing her to speak and acknowledge her own guilt, thinking there was no one near to hear it.

"Aidan? Please—who do you think runs his company?" Without waiting for an answer, Gisele plucked the syringe from the table, holding it poised above Colbie's arm.

"What about Gloria," Colbie asked, knowing her question would hit home. "It's no secret you've been skimming money from the cartel. Was that for personal use, Gisele? Or, were you sending it back to Cuba to use as they please?"

A glare, cueing Colbie she hit a nerve.

"And, what about Carmen Santosa," Colbie continued. "Is she next on your list?"

"Carmen Santosa has nothing to do with anything— she's merely a pawn. It's clear to anyone who isn't blind that Hector Cortina ruined her face, so it was easy to recruit her participation simply because she needed to satisfy her own needs. She was merely dropping intel to Hector—until he unfortunately died—then Analena, once her husband was no longer available, though it was only a couple of times." Gisele hesitated, as if considering something important. "I thought about ending Carmen's miserable life, too—but, I simply haven't gotten around to it."

"Why? If Carmen Santosa is nothing to you—"

"Oh, I'm sure if you think about it, you'll figure it out."

Colbie was silent for a second before looking Gisele in her eyes. "She's become a liability . . ."

"Excellent!"

"What about Gloria," Colbie asked for the second time.

Suddenly, Gisele's expression morphed into pure hatred, her grip on Colbie's arm strengthening. "Gloria Fuentes is hardly the cartel leader her father was—while he was alive, he and I had an agreement. He said nothing, and I stayed out of his hair—it was really quite simple and effective. A mutual respect, if you will . . ."

"Juan knew you were skimming?"

Again, Gisele glanced at the screen door, as if sensing something wasn't right. "Of course, he knew! He was the one who suggested it . . ."

"Why? Why would he sanction such a thing if it meant taking money out of his own pocket?"

A twisted grin. "Because he stood to make far more money from our transactions . . ."

"So, he flew under the radar while doing it," Colbie surmised, knowing she had all the answers she needed.

Saying nothing and with expert precision, Gisele tested the needle, squirting a small amount from the needle's tip, then held it to Colbie's best vein. "Say your goodbyes," Gisele suggested, pressing the needle against Colbie's arm.

Suddenly and without warning, the screen door burst open with enough force to knock it from its hinges. Decklin and Devon emerged from the darkness, Decklin training his weapon directly on Gisele's head. "Move away from her, Gisele!"

"Deck! She has a syringe!"

Heeding Colbie's warning and with adrenalin pumping, Devon dove across the cabin's floor, tackling Gisele at the knees, taking her down as he would a college wrestling opponent, not considering his injured arm. Struggling to gain advantage, Gisele raised the syringe above her head, her body writhing as she chanted unintelligible words, her eyes wild and maniacal. "You must die," she wailed as she tried to twist away from Devon's weight.

Straddling her as he attempted to grab her wrist, Devon put his weight on Gisele's right arm with his left knee, pressing into her with as much force as he could while latching onto her left wrist, shaking it violently. "Drop it!"

A choking laugh.

"Drop it, Gisele!" Then, with a force he rarely exhibited, Devon positioned his thumb at the base of her fingers, bending them until he heard bones crunch. "I said drop it!"

"'You will die," Gisele again bellowed, her voice low and deep, as if possessed by something dark. Something evil. Then, with inexplicable power and force, she knocked Devon's hand away, plunging the syringe anywhere it would land.

Jerking his right leg away from her body, Devon shifted just enough, allowing Decklin the opportunity he needed. With Gisele's head in view, he took his shot, placing a perfect 9 mil bullet between her eyes.

Eyes open, her hand dropped as blood oozed slightly from the bullet hole, the syringe stabbed into the cabin's floor. Then?

Silence.

"Thank you," Colbie suddenly whispered, fully realizing how close she came to closing her eyes for the last time.

Decklin glanced at Devon who knelt beside Gisele's body, his eyes the size of bread and butter plates. "You okay," he asked, scanning his partner from head-to-toe.

A nod. "I think so . . ."

Immediately, Decklin crossed to Colbie, kneeling in front of her as he fished for the pocket knife he had since he was twelve. Flicking it open, he cut the zip tie on her ankles, releasing its pressure. "What about you?"

"I'm fine—shaken, but fine. Again, thank you . . ."

Helping her stand, Decklin tucked his arm around her as he focused on Devon. "Call the authorities . . ."

CHAPTER 28

As Decklin suspected, it took Colbie Colleen approximately four seconds to process what happened, wanting to discuss it with Decklin the following morning—which worked out well since Decklin ordered Devon to get much needed rest. "How about if I come to you," Decklin suggested when he dropped her off at her hotel.

So, with plans made, the following morning he ordered room service before arriving, surprising Colbie with a breakfast of her dreams. "I hope you like salmon and eggs Benedict," he laughed, watching her close her eyes after her first bite.

"This is so good," she murmured, savoring what she considered a taste of home. "It reminds me of a place I used to go in Seattle . . ."

Then, it was down to business.

"How did you figure out where I was," Colbie asked, even though Decklin gave her a synopsis the prior evening.

"Well, when you didn't answer your phone—especially in light of the conversation we had at dinner the night before—I knew something was wrong." Decklin took a bite of salmon, chasing it with a sip of coffee as he cycled through exactly what happened. "I also recognized the area where Anderson was found—but, I knew it would be impossible for us to get past the tape."

"Anderson didn't want me to go . . ."

"That's what's missing for me—why were you there after our dinner?"

Colbie was silent for a moment, her fork poised over her plate. "Because I knew," she finally admitted, "if I were to have a relationship with you, I needed to say goodbye to Brian, and I wanted to do it somewhere other than a lifeless hotel room."

"So, you chose the beach where we met to discuss the case . . ."

A nod. "I'm sure Anderson wasn't happy with me— he wanted me to use my flashlight, but I didn't want to. Moonlight was enough as I walked the path to the beach . . ."

"How long were you there?"

"Not long—maybe twenty minutes."

Decklin reached across the round table, taking her hand in his. "Are you okay?"

Another nod. "With that, yes—but, it sickens me to think of Anderson, and it's my fault in some way because I asked him to take me there."

"I get it—losing a colleague is never easy. But, Gisele would've found another way to get to you . . ." Though Decklin never experienced losing a partner, he came close enough to know how it felt.

Squeezing his hand, Colbie freed hers to take a sip of orange juice. "So. The case . . . I told MPD I'll be available to speak with them by this afternoon."

"Good—Devon and I will do the same."

An unexpected silence before Decklin placed his napkin on his plate, then drained his coffee cup. "You know I'm falling in love with you, don't you?"

Colbie blushed, then patted her lips with her napkin. "I know . . ."

"So, where do we go from here," he asked, slightly disappointed Colbie didn't confess the same for him.

"Honestly, I don't know what's on my horizon—one thing I do know, however, is I'm not open to working another case where I'm embedded. I realize I much prefer working outside the confines of rules and regulations . . ."

"I know what you mean—that's exactly why I'm an unemployed private investigator now." Decklin sat back in his chair, eyeing her. "Will you go back to Seattle?"

"I doubt it—I might visit family for a while, but I don't think I'll settle there. Too many memories . . ."

Then, Decklin asked the question both of them dreaded. "What about us?"

Colbie shook her head. "I'm not sure—are you going to stay in Miami?"

An unexpected lull for a few moments as Decklin considered his future in southern climes—something he hadn't done until then. "Well, am I wild about the oppressive heat and humidity? No. Is it fair to leave Devon high and dry? No. But, I have to admit, I don't know the future—all I know is I want to have you in it. So, I guess that's the best answer I have, at least for now."

"You have a lot on the line, which makes it more difficult for you to decide. You have a lease on an office, not to mention a young partner who's willing to get his feet wet no matter what." Colbie hesitated, thinking of the days when Brian was at her side during investigations. "That's important . . ."

"I'm aware—so, I think it'll take a little time to figure out where I go from here." Again, Decklin took Colbie's hand, giving it an affectionate squeeze. "Or, where we go from here—I can't think of my life without you in it."

Returning the affection, Colbie smiled. "There's always risk required in everything we do—the crapshoot is how we handle those risks as well as to what end."

"Agreed—but, for now, we have business to attend to. I feel we need to attend Anderson's memorial service, if possible. It may well be only family will be allowed to attend and, if that's the case, I don't blame them . . ."

"Nor do I—but, on my end, I have loose ends to wrap up, and I need to make decisions about a few things. That's going to take some time . . ."

So, with all important things discussed, Decklin Kilgarry and Colbie Colleen sat in silence for a few minutes, each thinking private thoughts. If Decklin had his way, he'd make a life with the petite psychic investigator in a New York minute—the question was would she be as impetuous? A part of him hoped so, but until they were spending more time together, he wouldn't know if it were part of her personality. But, as Colbie mentioned, life wasn't without risk.

In fact, it's required.

CHAPTER 29

Of course, there were headlines and, though Colbie tried to keep her name out of the whole mess, it wasn't to be. But, after a week, interest died down, the media on to something more titillating.

"It's finally over," Devon commented as he and Decklin sat down for a meeting to discuss their future. "So, where do we go from here," Devon asked as he parked in one of two chairs in front of Decklin's desk.

But, before Decklin shared his thoughts, he needed to know what was swirling around in his partner's brain. "Where are you with it?"

"Well, I have to admit, everything that happened within the last few months scared the livin' shit out of me—and, now that it's over, I knew you'd ask that question."

"Do you have any answers," Decklin asked, keeping his focus on Devon. "I admit, you were thrown to the wolves—but, honestly, I don't see how it could've been any other way."

"I agree—so, over this past week, I've been assessing and reassessing, trying to figure out if I made the right decision." A grin as Devon sat forward in his chair, elbows on his knees. "And, I admit there's a part of me wanting the assurances of a wealthy life, yet I realize I'm suited to the investigations business. It's what makes my blood flow in the morning and, though it keeps me awake at night, I can't think of anything else I'd rather do."

"I know the feeling . . ."

"So, I say we continue our partnership—that's if you're up for it."

Decklin stood, extending his hand across the desk. "I was hoping you'd say that! Partners we are!"

Thrilled, Devon accepted the handshake. "Excellent! But, I have one more question, and you don't have to answer it if you don't want to . . ."

Taking his seat, Decklin nodded. "Shoot . . ."

"Where does Colbie fit into everything?" Of course, Devon had no doubt romance was brewing between the two, but figured it was none of his business until that moment.

"I'm glad you asked—we had a long discussion after everything went down, and both of us are keen on seeing where our relationship goes."

"What about her gig in Miami?"

"It's done—not because of the Feds, though. She decided she'd rather investigate according to her rules and regs, and not someone else's."

"I don't blame her—being your own boss has it perks. Will she go back to running her own show?"

"Maybe—she did say, however, she's not into handling all the frustration that goes with it. I think—though I'm not sure—she'll go forward solo."

Devon was silent as he focused on Decklin, unsure if he should voice his thoughts. "Well," he finally commented, "what do you think about her working with us? That's if she wants to, of course . . ."

Decklin said nothing, quickly weighing if such a thing were possible, considering whether Colbie's being a part of their investigative firm were a good idea. After all, chances of ruining their blossoming relationship had to be considered. "We can certainly talk to her about it . . ."

"Good—when?"

"I don't know her schedule, but, when we do, I think it's important you're in on all conversations . . ."

"Agreed. So, call her!"

"Now?"

"Yes! Why wait? We need to start on getting our next client, and not taking action is a great way to get behind on paying bills!"

Decklin stared at his young partner, wondering when he turned into a full-fledged adult. Deciding he was right, Decklin plucked his cell from his pocket, tapped the screen, then waited for Colbie to answer. A few minutes later?

A confab on the books.

Unfortunately, for the next ten days or so, Colbie's dance card was full as she took care of finishing Miami business. There were, however, loose ends needing attention . . .

Gloria Fuentes for one.

Finding her, however, was more difficult than originally anticipated. Speculation of Gloria's returning to Mexico mounted and was finally realized when the Feds made a dent in the cartel's Miami operations, arresting several for various charges including bank and wire fraud, among others.

Sans Gloria.

"It'll take years for her to be arrested for Manuel's murder and Devon's beat-down," Colbie commented as she, Decklin, and Devon met to discuss her joining their investigations team. "But, the one who really skated," she asked glancing at both of them, yet knowing her question was rhetorical. "Aidan Lopez."

"No charges for trafficking or anything else," Devon asked, stunned the justice system would look the other way.

"Nope—not one. I sense the Feds are more interested in other players such as Gloria, et al. I'm sure they'll find other charges to slap on her and, when she's finally extradited to

Miami, her days as cartel queen will effectively be over. So, in the meantime, Aidan skates . . ."

"What about the treason aspect of our case," Decklin asked, reaching for the restaurant-style coffee carafe. "What about Amelia Sandoval since she was in on it?"

"Well, that's interesting—she may be considered a witness. Or, since she passed intel, she may be on the hot seat and indicted for something. I also feel it would be for a crime lesser than treason. But, I think she was more interested in the Santeria part of it—and, we can't really prove she was passing information since Thomas is dead. So, I suspect she'll be free to continue her spiritual preferences . . ."

"And, Analena?"

Colbie glanced at Decklin, then focused on Devon. "Well, I don't see she's guilty of anything—all she wanted to do was find out if her husband were cheating. She did, however, pass intel a couple of times that we know of, so I'm not too sure . . ."

"Carmen Santosa?"

"Indictment material—but, she had no idea about the intel content. All she did was drop it in the dark and, as far as we can tell, nothing else."

So, for the next fifteen, they hashed out particulars regarding their case, finally putting it to bed. "Now," Decklin began, "we have a proposition for you . . ."

"That sounds interesting," Colbie laughed, topping off her coffee cup. "But, I already know," she admitted. "And, my answer is yes . . ."

"Of course, you already knew," Decklin laughed, raising his coffee cup for a toast.

Blushing, Colbie raised her cup. "As I said, there's always a risk—without it, we'd be bored as hell!"

"To risk required," Devon chimed in as the new investigative team toasted its future—optimistic, each knew their lives were about to change.

"And," Colbie offered, "it just so happens I may have our next case lined up—if you agree, of course!"

Decklin glanced at his partner, a familiar glint in his eye. "Okay—spill!"

"Oh, no! Not yet—but, when I know more, you two will be the first to know!"

"Can you give us a hint," Devon asked, hoping he didn't need to resort to pleading.

Thinking for a moment, Colbie smiled. "Okay, but just one—and, it's only two words." Pausing, she enjoyed their curiosity, knowing their partnership was about to be tested.

"Doomsday clock . . ."

NOVELS BY FAITH WOOD

COLBIE COLLEEN SUSPENSE MYSTERY SERIES

The Accidental Audience—Book 1
Chasing Rhinos—Book 2
Apology Accepted—Book 3
Whiskey Snow—Book 4
Chill of Deception—Book 5
At the Intersection of Blood and Money—Book 6
The Scent of Unfinished Business—Book 7
Agenda—Book 8

DECKLIN KILGARRY SUSPENSE MYSTERY SERIES

Where Truth Goes to Die—Book 1
SOHO—Book 2
Masterclass—Book 3
The Social Hour—Book 4

LAUNCHING IN SPRING 2024!

Risk Required
A Decklin Kilgarry and Colbie Collen Suspense Mystery Trilogy—Book 1

Professional Acknowledgments

CHRYSALIS PUBLISHING AUTHOR SERVICES
L.A. O'NEIL/EDITOR
www.chrysalis-pub.com
chrysalispub@gmail.com

Manufactured by Amazon.ca
Bolton, ON

36681325R00160